"I'll be gentle with you," she said

Eric cleared his throat and tried not to make anything of the way Dallas was moistening her lips. Tried not to stare at her glistening lower lip. "Not *too* gentle. That would take out all the excitement."

Her eyebrows rose.

Eric smiled. "Bring it on."

She laughed, deep and throaty, the sound skating down his spine. "You're giving me carte blanche?"

"I'm all yours."

"Hmm..."

She bit her lip. And it was tempting, he thought, incredibly tempting. She liked him. The chemistry was certainly there. This is obviously what she wanted.

He moved closer. She didn't retreat. Excellent sign. "So what would you like to do with me?"

"Oh, I never tip my hand too soon."

"Oh, right. A woman of mystery and surprise."

"You have no idea."

Blaze™

Dear Reader,

One of the most common questions I'm asked is where do I get my ideas? The first time I was asked this I had trouble answering. The ideas just come to me, usually unbidden. They're kind of always there, lurking, waiting to be triggered by the most obscure thing. My imagination just doesn't quit. *A Glimpse of Fire* is a perfect example.

I live in Las Vegas, where imagination seems to run amok. One evening I took visiting friends to The Venetian, an Italian-themed casino where they have gondola rides and an "outdoor" courtyard designed to look like a quaint Italian village complete with white-faced, costumed street mimes. I wasn't sure the first one I saw was a real person. I caught a glimpse of movement and then stared for the longest time waiting for the next flicker. A dollar tossed in the bowl at his feet earned a slight nod. That was it. And so the idea for this book wouldn't let go.

Hope you enjoy Eric and Dallas's ride. Hang on!

Best,

Debbi Rawlins

Books by Debbi Rawlins

HARLEQUIN BLAZE

*Men To Do

DEBBI RAWLINS

A GLIMPSE OF FIRE

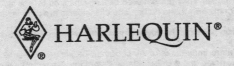

HARLEQUIN®

TORONTO • NEW YORK • LONDON
AMSTERDAM • PARIS • SYDNEY • HAMBURG
STOCKHOLM • ATHENS • TOKYO • MILAN • MADRID
PRAGUE • WARSAW • BUDAPEST • AUCKLAND

This is for Steve and E. I'm so glad you found each other.
You're everything I write about.

ISBN 0-373-79187-9

A GLIMPSE OF FIRE

_1_

DALLAS SHEA CHECKED HER WATCH and then shoved her keys and two twenties into her jeans pocket. She'd planned on walking the eighteen blocks up midtown but now she had to catch a cab or she'd be late.

"Oh, good, you're still here." Her roommate burst out of the tiny bathroom they shared while she pulled her long red hair up into a ponytail. Behind her a heap of towels lay near the foot of the ancient claw-foot tub.

Dallas sighed. The woman was the consummate slob. Funny, spontaneous, ambitious and a loyal friend but a total slob. "Not for long. I'm on my way out."

"Can you walk Bruiser first?"

"No."

The furry black mutt heard his name and came from behind the green floral couch, which was the extent of their tiny living room, wagging his tail, looking up at Dallas with soulful black eyes. He had to be up to seven pounds by now—big difference from three months ago, when Wendy found him scrounging for food in an alley near Nineteenth Street.

"Please, Dallas. I'll make dinner."

Giving Wendy a dry look, Dallas headed for the door,

trying to avoid looking at Bruiser. If she did, she'd give in. "That's what you said the last time."

"I came through, didn't I?"

"Hot dogs from Howie's cart is not my idea of dinner."

"Come on, please. I have an audition." Wendy hopped on one leg as she pulled on a tennis shoe over her purple tights. "It's really important. A new musical and they need twelve dancers. This time I'm going to get it. I know it. Right here." She pressed a palm to her tummy. "This is gonna be my big break."

Dallas undid the dead bolt. Then hesitated, reminding herself this wasn't her business. But Wendy was crazy for chasing after these jobs. Sadly, at twenty-nine, she was already too old for Broadway. A new crop of eager, energetic young twenty-somethings were getting all the gigs.

She looked at her friend and then down at Bruiser, whose expectant eyes met hers, his tail still wagging. Even he'd already figured out what a pushover Dallas was.

Sighing, she opened the door for Wendy. "Go."

Grinning, Wendy hopped toward her as she slid on her other sneaker. "You're the best."

"Be careful of those feet. I need your share of the rent." Dallas scooped up Bruiser before he made a break for the open door, then grabbed his leash off the hook on the wall. "Don't worry about dinner. I'm meeting Trudie."

"Tell her I said hey."

"Break a leg," Dallas said as Wendy slipped out into the hall and closed the door.

She put Bruiser down and crouched to secure his leash. "What are you looking at me like that for? Huh?" She stroked his curly black fur, laughed when he licked her chin, rearing back just in the nick of time to avoid a sloppy kiss.

"Okay, boy, I know it's been a while since I've had a date but I like my guys a little taller." She stood, grabbing the plastic bag she needed to clean up after Bruiser.

In a way she envied Wendy. She never gave up. Her optimism and enthusiasm seemed boundless. Even after she'd lost the contract with Revalyn last year. A week after her twenty-eighth birthday, the company decided they needed someone with younger-looking hands for their print ads. Thank God feet didn't age as quickly.

Dallas sighed. Boy, was she glad she'd gotten out of that world quickly. She'd modeled for a year during her senior year in college. After the blowup with her parents when they'd cut her off, she'd needed the money. But that had been enough. There had always been someone taller, slimmer, prettier. She'd hated every minute of it.

She led Bruiser out of the apartment, careful to double lock the door, then checked her watch as she waited for the elevator, hoping the damn thing wasn't on a milk run. Of course, that it was working at all was cause for celebration. If she had the money, she'd move out, but finding and affording another apartment without having to move to Brooklyn would mean working a whole lot of overtime. Or worse, taking another job. The kind her parents would approve. The thought made her shudder.

"THANK GOD YOU'RE HERE." Trudie looked up from a pink phone slip on her desk, her heavily outlined brown eyes filled with worry. "Close the door, would you?"

"Sure." Dallas did as asked and then dropped into the worn burgundy leather guest chair. "What's up?"

"I'm totally screwed."

Dallas tried not to smile. Her friend had a penchant for drama. Their circle of college friends had been certain Trudie would end up on Broadway and not dressing department store windows. "What's wrong?"

"I'm in charge of doing the Fifth Avenue window display for the Fourth of July sale. It's also the store's tenth anniversary."

"Sounds like a big deal."

"Yes," Trudie said miserably. "And I'm about to blow it big-time."

"How?"

Trudie shoved the pink slip she'd been studying across her crowded desk, between a stack of fashion magazines and a pile of fabric swatches.

Dallas picked up the phone message. It was from someone named Starla Jenkins. It simply said she had a stomach virus and had to cancel tomorrow evening.

"Okay," Dallas said slowly, sliding the pink slip back toward Trudie. Her friend was obviously upset, so she forwent the wisecrack that came to mind. "And?"

"I am so screwed."

"Who's Starla Jenkins?"

"A model I'd hired." Trudie exhaled sharply. "Stom-

ach virus, my ass. I haven't heard of anything going around."

"So? I'm sure there are fifteen others who'd love to take her place. Call the agency."

"It's not that simple," Trudie said and then remained silent as she stared at Dallas with an odd expression on her face. Her gaze dropped to Dallas's hands and she wrinkled her nose. "Your nails are horrible."

Dallas reflexively balled them into fists. "I just got off work."

"That's okay." Trudie flashed her a quick smile. "We can fix them."

"I don't want them fixed." She studied her friend for a moment, a bad feeling growing in the pit of her stomach. "Look, if you need to cancel dinner so you can find a replacement, I totally understand."

Trudie's gaze stayed steady. "I already have."

Dallas stared back, feeling uneasy. Trudie couldn't possibly be thinking— No, of course not. Ridiculous. She knew better. But just in case… "No."

"Come on, Dallas. I'm not asking you to do it for free."

"Why ask me period? You could find a replacement in half an hour."

"No way, toots." Trudie shook her head. "I promised my manager something special. A live mannequin."

Dallas's mouth opened but didn't cooperate any further.

"*You* gave me the idea," Trudie said in an accusatory tone. "Remember how in college you used to fake everyone out. Jill and I'd take bets you could stay perfectly still for a half hour at a time. Hell, we used to clean up. Pay for all our gas and entertainment."

"That was eight years ago."

"You did it again at the Christmas party last year and took fifty bucks off that snobby Chandler Whitestone."

"That was different. He ticked me off."

"Please, Dallas. You have to bail me out."

Dallas sighed. Did she have *Sucker* written across her forehead or something? "I have faith you'll find someone else. Or come up with another window display."

"By tomorrow?"

"I'm not standing in a damn department store window. I'm too out of shape."

"Bull. You should have never left the business." Trudie glanced at Dallas's hands again. "Your nails suck, but other than that you're every bit as pretty and—"

"I'm twenty-nine."

Trudie's mouth twisted wryly. "There's that."

Dallas stood. "Moot point. Are we doing dinner or not?"

"Look, my career's on the line here." Trudie hesitated. "I wouldn't ask if I wasn't desperate."

"Have you *even tried* to find someone else?"

"Yes. I swear."

Dallas sank back into the chair. She believed her. Trudie wasn't one to ask for favors. Even after her jerk of a boyfriend had moved out along with half of Trudie's furniture and the next month's rent, she hadn't asked Dallas or Wendy for a thing. Hadn't accepted anything that was offered either.

"Come on, Dallas. As soon as Starla gets over her virus or whatever, she'll call and you'll be off the hook."

"I'm not on the hook."

"Oh, God, are you going to make me beg? Do I have to get down on my knees?"

Dallas sighed, knowing she was going to regret this. "Okay," she said slowly. "How long do I have to pose and what do I have to wear?"

Trudie's smile faltered. "Come on, let's go have a drink or two first."

"Trudie…"

Her friend got up from her desk, grabbed her purse and headed out the door. "I'm buying."

Dallas followed. She was not going to like this. Not one bit.

ERIC HARMON PAID THE cabdriver and got out near Sixth and Lexington. No sign of Tom. He checked his watch. Traffic had been surprisingly cooperative, and he'd apparently beaten his friend to the rendezvous point a block from their office where they both worked for Webber and Thornton Advertising.

He squinted up at the twentieth floor and counted four windows from the corner, which was Tom's office. The light was still on. But of course, so was the light in Eric's office, two over from Tom's, and Eric had no intention of returning to work. Not today. He was too beat.

They really should've met at Pete's Grille, he realized. After the meeting he had just left, he could really use a double scotch about now. He checked his watch again, moved out of the way as a horde of pedestrians left the crosswalk and headed for him, then withdrew his cell phone from his suit jacket pocket.

"Put that away. I'm right behind you."

He turned toward Tom's voice and slid the phone back into his pocket. "I need a drink."

"Me, too."

Eric looked down at the briefcase his friend was holding. "Since when do you take work home?"

Tom shook his head, his expression grim. "I don't care how bad your meeting went, be damn glad you weren't in the office this afternoon."

"Great. Tell me it doesn't have to do with the Mercer account." The advertising business could be a bitch. When you bonded with the client, you were on top of the world. But then there were those times when you thought about ordering a one-way ticket to Siberia.

"I'm not talking work until after I have a scotch." Tom stepped back, accidentally bumping into a short blonde in a khaki suit. "Excuse me."

At his dimpled smile, her irritation promptly vanished. "No problem." She returned the smile, laced with a brief but obvious invitation.

Eric sighed. "Come on, Romeo. Let's get to Pete's before your wife calls and tells you to get your ass home."

Tom gave the blonde's swaying rear end a final appreciative look before turning toward Fourth Avenue. "Speaking of wives, since *you* don't have one—" Tom said as if it were a crime "—who are you taking to We ber's annual thanks-for-the-job-well-done-but-you're-not-getting-a-bonus party?"

"Who says I have to take anyone?"

"Unspoken rule, my friend. You always show up and you don't show up alone. The guy's old school. He thinks everyone should be married and settled by the time they're thirty. A mark you've already bypassed. Besides, didn't you get the picture after the Christmas party? He didn't like it that you were the only one flying solo."

Eric scoffed. "That attitude's not only ridiculously antiquated, it's illegal."

"Tell him that." Tom's head swung around after a red-headed jogger in a skintight green tank and running shorts who'd passed them.

"And then there are some guys who just shouldn't be married."

"What?" Tom glanced at him and laughed. "Only looking, pal. Only looking. Something you should be doing more of."

Frankly he didn't know how Tom did it. Juggle a wife, a successful but demanding career and an active and strategic social life. Of course, Tom's first putt in life came with a handicap. Prominent Westchester family. Ivy League education. No student loans to repay. A wife with an impressive social pedigree.

Must be nice. Eric wouldn't know. His background was Pittsburgh blue-collar all the way. Of his entire extended family, he'd been the first to graduate from college and escape a life sweating in the steel mills.

"Seriously, Eric," he continued, "when was the last time you brought someone to a company function?"

"Why are we discussing this?"

"Tell me when and I'll drop it."

"Why would I subject a date to one of Webber's boring parties?" He was about to cross the street when the light turned red. Normally that wouldn't stop him, except a stretch limo came barreling around the corner from Lexington.

"See? Good reason to get married. Then the girl's gotta go and be bored."

"Right."

Tom elbowed him. "Check out the blonde at three o'clock. The one in the red stiletto heels."

Eric casually glanced in that direction. "Not bad."

"Not bad? Are you nuts? That one could put you in intensive care for a month."

Eric started to cross the street as soon as the light changed. Two cabs ran the red light and honked at the pedestrians who'd entered the crosswalk. Across the street several other cabs blasted their horns for no apparent reason. You'd never know the city imposed a three-hundred-fifty-dollar fine for unnecessary honking.

They'd barely made it across Fifth Avenue when Tom started in again. "Okay, I want you to point out your idea of the perfect woman." He gestured toward the mass of people, mostly women in suits and running shoes, coming toward them. "You have a wide variety right here."

"What is with you today?"

"Humor me."

Eric shook his head in disgust, at the same time catching sight of a department store window display, taken aback by the realistic beach scene. Sand, sun, a threatening wave that looked as if it were about to crash over two incredibly lifelike mannequins and then right through the window onto the sidewalk. Computer generated, obviously, but realistic enough to earn some gasps from the crowd of onlookers and send an older couple back several steps.

Remarkable as the special effects were, what caught his attention was the blond mannequin in the red bikini. She looked so damn real. And perfect. Long honey-blond hair, sexy blue eyes, full lips that formed a tempting bow. And man did she have legs....

"Are you listening?" Tom got in his face.

"What?" Eric hadn't realized he'd stopped. Right in the middle of the sidewalk, blocking everyone's way. People muttered curses and stepped around him. "No."

He looked back at the window. At the mannequin. She was amazing. Incredible. Too bad that kind of perfection could only be synthetic.

Tom followed his gaze just as another wave swelled threateningly, and he ducked. Clearly realizing his foolish reaction, he straightened and glanced around. Several other onlookers had done the same.

"Damn, that's amazing."

Eric nodded. "Genius. Pure genius. Look at how many people the window's attracting."

"No shit. This should earn someone a nice little bonus."

Eric shook his head. Lately with Tom it was always about money or women. As if he needed to worry about either. "Let's go."

"Wait. No more changing the subject. You have an assortment of lovelies right here. Blondes, brunettes, redheads." Ignoring a sharp look he received from a well-dressed older woman who'd obviously overheard, he gestured toward a group staring at the window. "I'm not moving until you choose one."

Eric shrugged and turned to leave. "I'll say hey to everyone at Pete's for you."

Tom snagged his coat sleeve. "Come on."

Eric sighed. His gaze went back to the mannequin, to the tiny beauty mark at the corner of her lush mouth. "Her," he said with a jut of his chin.

"Who?" Tom scanned the group of women close to the window. "Which one?"

"There." Eric barely contained a smile as he fixed his gaze on the mannequin. "She's perfect."

It took Tom a moment for it to register and then he laughed. "Why, because she can't talk?"

"A big bonus, you have to admit."

"I'll give you that." Tom studied the mannequin. "Great legs, too. I wonder if she's busy this weekend."

Eric shook his head and headed across the street. "I'm gonna go have a drink. You do what you want."

Tom started after him when he heard the crowd gasp. He turned just in time to see the two mannequins throwing their hands up as if frightened by the wave, and then they repositioned themselves, again going perfectly still.

The crowd began murmuring and talking excitedly, loud enough that Eric turned around to see what was happening. Tom took off after him.

"What's going on?" Eric asked.

"Nothing. Another wave." Tom shouldered him, urging him to keep walking. "Let's go before my keeper calls."

Tom could barely contain himself. This was rich. Totally awesome. He wasn't sure what he was going to do yet, but the opportunity for something really big was there.

Like Saturday night—the company dinner. God, this was too perfect.

In his excitement, he nearly tripped over his own feet.

All he had to do was keep Eric away from that window for the next two days.

2

TEN MORE MINUTES. FIFTEEN tops, and the store would be closing, judging by the steady stream of shoppers exiting the Fifth Avenue doors. She could do this. Wait fifteen minutes before she sprinted to the bathroom. Dallas simply had to stop thinking about how her bladder was ready to explode.

Even though she'd purposely laid off the coffee and Cokes made available in the dressing room, the knowledge that she was stuck in the window and couldn't leave was enough to make her desperate for a pit stop. One five-minute break in four hours just didn't cut it. She and Trudie were going to have a serious discussion tomorrow.

Dallas heard her partner's stomach growl and used every ounce of self-control to keep a straight face. Steve did an admirable job of remaining impassive himself, and she kept her gaze fixed on the fire hydrant across the street. It was easier that way, to focus on one particular object until the soft beep told them it was time to change positions. Besides, making eye contact with anyone in the crowd outside wasn't a good idea. Made it much harder to keep a straight face and not blink.

She'd almost blown it earlier. Two yuppies had stopped and stared, obviously more interested in her bikini than the window display. The taller one had caught her eye with his dark wavy hair and light eyes and a tanned face with a deep cleft in his strong chin that had a way of sending her thoughts in a dangerous direction.

The announcement came that the store would be closing in five minutes.

Freedom. Hallelujah!

She and Steve exchanged a brief glance.

That's when she noticed him. Approaching the window. One of the guys she'd seen earlier. Not the good-looking one with the dimpled chin but the shorter one.

He stopped dead center and stared at her intensely, thoroughly, as if she were a museum exhibit. She tried not to move, not to give any sign of acknowledgement. Then he mouthed something to her, but still she refused to focus on his lips or try to understand what he was saying.

Panic knotted her tummy, and she tried to disguise the deep unsteady breath she took. Just what she needed—some pervert following her home later. She'd have to duck out the employee door, maybe even get Steve to share a cab with her.

The guy walked up to the security guard, who stood at the door making sure no one slipped inside, and the two men shook hands. They apparently knew each other, which brought Dallas some relief.

Behind her, Trudie's assistant opened the door to the window, at the same time dimming the display lights, a signal it was over. They were free. At least until tomorrow night. She and Steve looked at each other. He smiled. She groaned. Of course, he looked as if he were barely out of his teens. His back and legs probably didn't ache as hers did.

"You okay?" he asked, his incredibly pretty blue eyes clouding with genuine concern. Nice guy. Idaho born and bred, he'd only moved to the city six months ago. He'd change. They all did.

"Terrific."

"You look awful."

"Thank you."

"I didn't mean it like that." He actually blushed as he stepped aside to let her out first.

She grinned. Too bad he wasn't older. "Aren't you a little stiff?"

His brows rose in surprise. "Why?"

"Never mind."

She climbed out, smiling ruefully to herself. It wasn't that she was in bad shape. Just the opposite. Working in construction for the past year and a half had probably gotten her into the best condition she'd ever been. This was different. Holding the same position for an hour at a time wasn't easy. Nothing like it had been eight years ago in college.

A couple of stragglers leaving the store stopped to stare at her. She accepted a robe from Trudie's assistant and pulled it on over the tiny red bikini before heading for the dressing room. The lights flickered—the store's final warning for everyone to leave.

"Hey, you wanna go for a drink?" Steve threw his robe over his shoulder.

Drink? Bathroom? Oh, God. "How about a rain check?" she said without breaking her stride.

"Sure." He shrugged, smiled. "See you tomorrow evening."

Dallas sighed as he walked ahead of her. He sure was pretty. Young but pretty.

"Excuse me."

Dallas heard the voice behind her and glanced over her shoulder. It was him. The guy who'd been standing outside a moment ago. Her chest tightened. "The store is closed. You'll have to leave."

He gave her a boyish grin. "I know the security guard. Besides, I only need a minute of your time."

"I don't have a minute."

"Look, I want to hire you." He produced a business card from his jacket pocket. "For Saturday night. Your usual modeling fee, of course."

She barely glanced at the card. "I'm not a model. I'm doing this as a favor for a friend." She tried to hand him back the card but he wouldn't take it.

"Call my office," he said. "Check me out. Or ask Jimmy." He inclined his head toward the security guard.

She shook her head. "Look, I—"

"I'm not a kook or a pervert." His boyish grin took a chink out of her resolve. "Well, my friends may argue that point. But seriously, I only want to play a practical joke on my friend. He was here earlier with me and saw and…well, we have a company dinner at the boss's house this Saturday and I thought it would be pretty funny if you showed up."

Of course she remembered the guy. His face was surprisingly clear in her mind. That strong, dimpled jaw stood out in particular.

"He thinks you're a mannequin."

That startled a laugh out of her. Oops! Bad move. She squeezed her thighs together. "I'll think about it and call you, okay?" she said as she started toward the bathroom.

"Tom!" The security guard motioned the man to the door. "I gotta lock up."

"I'll be waiting to hear from you." Tom backed toward the door. "Either way, call me, will you?"

"Sure," she said, amazed that she was even considering it.

"I THINK YOU'RE NUTS IF YOU *don't* go." Wendy plopped down on the love seat with a bowl of buttered popcorn that she placed between her thighs. "How totally cool. You'd be like the mystery woman."

If Dallas denied being intrigued by the prospect, she'd be a liar, but the situation was just so way out there. "Pass me some popcorn, would you?"

"You won't like it. I used a whole block of butter," she said, licking her fingers.

"I don't suppose you set any popcorn aside for me."

"Sorry."

"Thanks." Dallas sighed as she pushed off the purple beanbag chair. Some things never changed.

They'd been roommates for three years, but Wendy

still hadn't grasped the concept of sharing. She had other good qualities, Dallas reminded herself as she grabbed an apple from the basket of fruit they kept on top of the refrigerator—the only spare spot in the minuscule kitchen.

"So, you saw this guy, right?" Wendy asked between handfuls of popcorn.

"Briefly. Anyway, it's not like it's a blind date. Just a prank."

"What does he look like?"

"Tall, kind of wiry, athletic-type body, dark hair, hazel eyes, strong square jaw."

Wendy snorted. "Just a brief look, huh?"

"Keep stuffing your face and shut up." Dallas sank back into the chair and stretched her legs out. "I called that guy Tom's office. I didn't talk to him. Just made sure he really worked there."

"And what about Saturday night? How do you know it's legit?"

"I pretended I was a florist and wanted to confirm the delivery date for the dinner."

"Very sneaky. I'm impressed."

Dallas groaned. "But I still don't know if I should do this."

"Did Trudie have an opinion?"

"Please, you need to ask? She thinks I'd be crazy to do it."

"Screw it. She's gotten too conservative since she caved in and got a nine-to-fiver. Go. Be daring. Have fun. What else do you have to do Saturday, anyway?"

Dallas watched a popcorn kernel slip from Wendy's hand and fall to the floor to join several of its friends. Dallas sighed. Wendy was right. What else did she have to do Saturday night besides clean up Wendy's mess?

ERIC FINISHED HIS COGNAC and debated having another one before he slipped out. As usual he'd come late, forgoing the cocktail hour and arriving just minutes before dinner had been served, along with a different wine with each course. Easy to get stupid with all that booze. And he made it a policy never to get stupid in front of the brass.

Webber, of course, was here. It was his house. He always threw the parties. New money. He still had a lot of showing off to do. The firm's other partner, Joseph Thornton IV, came from old money. Nice guy, old-school polite, but with the exception of Webber, no one from the office had ever seen the inside of his house. At least no one Eric knew of. Not that he was the type to be invited to the Thornton estate. But some day...hell, some day he'd have a nice three-story brownstone like this with a view of Central Park.

Near the white marble fireplace, Tom and Serena were talking to Harold Carter, the company's controller and possibly the most boring human being in Manhattan. Eric wasn't in the mood to make small talk, so he circled around the room, heading for the bar.

"Another cognac?" The bartender reached for the bottle.

"Yep, one for the road." Eric put down his empty

snifter. Most bartenders had amazing memories. "Go ahead and refill this one."

He'd picked up a clean glass but set it aside. "No argument from me. One less to wash."

Eric glanced at the guy's name tag. He remembered him from the Webber's Christmas party. "Tell me something, Chuck. You ever get tired of these private parties?"

Chuck shrugged. "They aren't so bad. Pays the rent."

Eric sighed. "Yep, that's what it's all about." He surveyed the plush living room, impeccably decorated in gold and burgundy, a van Gogh over the fireplace and, if he wasn't mistaken, a couple of Gauguins on the dining room wall. He hated these affairs. Ridiculously formal and mandatory—unspoken, of course. "Money."

Chuck grinned. "Nothing wrong with that."

"Not a thing." Eric had to agree. Not to would make him a hypocrite. Wasn't that why he was here when he'd rather be just about anyplace else? Not just because he was the only guest without a date—something which Webber had again commented on. But that was Eric's choice. He could have brought a date if he'd wanted.

Most of the time he could be political and schmooze the bosses with the best of them. He certainly did his share when necessary. Frankly he had to. It was all part of the game. But social situations weren't his favorite milieu. He always felt at such a disadvantage.

"The class of people at these private affairs are better than working the bars." Chuck motioned with his chin toward the foyer. "Like her. What a knockout! Can't believe I didn't notice her earlier."

Eric looked in that direction and saw the blonde entering the foyer. The Webber's maid had just let her in the double glass front doors. No escort. Just her and that slinky black dress.

She turned in his direction and his jaw dropped. That face. Those lips. That tiny beauty mark near her mouth. Those legs. He knew her....

Impossible.

He blinked. Took a deep shuddering breath. Exhaled slowly.

Chuck muttered an oath. "Sorry, man, I hope that isn't your wife or anything."

"What?" Eric barely glanced at the bartender before his gaze drew helplessly back to the woman. "No, I, um, I don't know her."

"In that case, I'd go introduce myself if I were you, dude." Chuck grabbed a crystal flute and poured some champagne. "Here. Take this to her."

Eric didn't move. He just stared. Blinked hard. Stared again. In total shock. The woman's resemblance to the mannequin he'd seen three days ago was remarkable. The hair on the back of his neck went straight up as he watched her enter the living room and take Mrs. Webber's extended hand.

"I need a scotch," he said to Chuck, his eyes never leaving the woman.

"Hey, dude, you okay?"

No, he wasn't okay. He was friggin' hallucinating. He finished his cognac and set it aside as he waited for Chuck to pour the scotch, and then he downed it in one gulp.

Tom.

Eric peered toward the marble fireplace where he'd last seen his friend. Where the hell was he? Tom had seen her in the window the other night, too. He could prove Eric wasn't going crazy.

Eric left the empty glass on the bar and moved toward the fireplace area while trying to keep the blonde in his sights. Wasn't hard. Everyone else seemed to be eyeing her, too. Of course, all the other guests knew each other. But it wasn't just that she was an outsider. She was stunning.

He spotted Tom, but before he could get to him, the blonde and Mrs. Webber approached him and his wife. Tom and Serena shook hands with the blonde. Not a trace of recognition on Tom's face.

Eric took a step back. Obviously he'd been working too hard lately. He was losing it. He needed to sit down. Have another drink. Better yet, go home.

"Hey, Eric. Come here." Tom motioned him toward them. "I'd like you to meet someone."

The blonde smiled. Her teeth were dazzlingly white and perfect. So was her skin. Flawless. Golden and creamy. And her honey-colored hair…the way the light from the chandelier touched it, lighting it with shimmering highlights, was a work of art.

A tiny half-moon-shaped scar near her jawline surprised him. Nothing bad or ugly but certainly unnecessary. A cosmetic surgeon could probably eliminate the imperfection with a thirty-minute office visit.

Too late to retreat gracefully, Eric moved forward and forced a smile.

Mrs. Webber leaned over and straightened his tie. "Don't leave too soon, okay? I have a very special dessert planned," she said with a twinkle in her eyes before drifting across the room.

"This is Eric Harmon," Tom said to the woman. "And Eric, this is Dallas."

She smiled and extended her hand. Eric's palm was so clammy, he was embarrassed to touch her. He took her fingers and brought her hand to his lips, pressing a light kiss to the back, which earned a choked snicker out of Tom.

"A pleasure meeting you," Eric said and released her hand as quickly as he could without seeming rude.

She blinked, surprise flickering across her face. "The pleasure is mine," she whispered, her voice soft and breathy and matching her perfectly.

The heady scent of roses and mystery swarmed his senses and he actually felt weak in the knees. His lips tingled from the silky warmth of her skin.

Too much scotch. That's all.

He caught the tail end of the amused look Tom and Serena had exchanged and he cleared his throat. "Tom, could I speak with you for a moment in private?"

Tom hesitated. Long enough for their boss, Morgan Webber, to call for Tom and motion for him across the room.

"Sorry, pal," Tom said, looking anything but as he hurried across the room toward Webber, Serena in tow.

Eric took a deep breath and turned back to Dallas. Her long, delicate fingers absently stroked the gold chain she wore around her neck. It held a small ruby heart that followed the deep V of her dress and rested in the tantalizing valley between her breasts.

He tried his damnedest not to stare. Forced his gaze up to the slender column of her neck, to her lush peach-tinted lips, the cute upward tilt of her nose and then to dive headfirst into eyes so sexy and blue, he thought he might have to loosen his collar to breathe.

He cleared his throat. "It's nice to see a new face at one of these parties. They get pretty stale after a while." He stopped, swore under his breath. "Tell me you aren't the Webbers' niece."

She smiled and shook her head.

"Or in any way related."

This time she laughed, the simple innocent sound seductive as hell. "No, you're safe."

Eric exaggerated a sigh of relief and then smiled. Up close he realized the scar on her jaw wasn't that old. Maybe a year or so. At least he knew she was a real live person.

God, he was losing it. He had to talk to Tom. Or then again, maybe he shouldn't. His friend was likely to have him committed. "How do you know the Webbers?"

Dallas looked blankly at him for a moment. And then her gaze shifted past him. "Would you get that waiter's attention, please? I'd really like a glass of wine."

"Of course." Damn, he should've brought the champagne Chuck had poured.

Eric snagged the waiter's attention. On his tray he had both white and red wine and flutes of champagne. Eric turned back to her to ask which she preferred and was surprised to find her nibbling nervously at her lower lip.

Their eyes met, and her lips immediately stretched into a smile, her expression one of utter composure.

"Red, white or champagne?" he asked.

"Red, thank you."

He lifted the glass off the tray and handed it to her. He thought about having another drink himself but decided he needed a clear head to survive the twilight zone.

"At the risk of sounding tedious, have we met before?" he asked and then waited for her to finish her sip.

She lowered the glass, and a tiny droplet of wine shimmered from her upper lip. Battling the urge to lick it was bad enough, but when she pursed her mouth, her lips forming a tempting pout, he totally lost his train of thought. What the hell had they been talking about?

"I'm sure I would remember," she said finally.

"Oh, yeah, right. Me, too." He should have had another drink. Never had he been so tongue-tied or at such a loss for words with a woman. "I mean, Dallas is an unusual name."

"Not in my family. My sister's name is Dakota. My brother's name is Cody."

"I'm sensing a pattern."

Her lips curved in a wry smile. "Very astute."

He smiled back. "Cody isn't so unusual."

"Not now. Thirty-three years ago it was, and he hated it with a passion."

"Ah, he must be your much older brother."

Laughter sparkled in her eyes. "*Much* older."

He guessed she was in her midtwenties, not that it mattered. "Where do you fall in the pecking order? Middle?"

Her eyebrows rose, and she seemed a little annoyed. "Does it show?"

Eric shrugged. "I haven't been around you long enough to know."

She didn't say anything but sipped her wine, still looking a little put off.

He understood her touchiness, which he wisely didn't point out. As far as he was concerned, whoever had come up with the "middle child syndrome" theory was on to something. He knew firsthand. "I'm right smack in the middle myself. A brother three years older and one three years younger. Both pains in the ass."

Her smile returned. "But you love them anyway."

"Yep, though I admit I don't always like them."

"Amen."

"We have something in common then."

Her voice lowering to a husky pitch, she said, "I wonder what else we have in common."

He took another sip of scotch. This had to be a joke. She was too perfect. And she'd just handed him the perfect opening. "How about we find out over dinner sometime?"

She blinked, uncertainty flitting across her face.

Eric silently cleared his throat. Had he misread the signal? Had he screwed up? It wasn't as if he'd been pushy. "Look, I—"

The lights flickered once, twice.

The room quieted for a few seconds, until the tinkling sound of metal meeting crystal broke the silence.

"May I have your attention?" Mrs. Webber stood with a crystal goblet in one hand and a silver spoon in the other. "I'd like you all to return to the table. We have a special dessert we're about to serve."

Great. Just how he wanted to spend the next hour. Eric turned back to Dallas.

She was gone.

3

AFTER EVERYONE WAS SEATED, the lights went out and two waiters carried trays of flaming Baked Alaska high above their heads into the dining room. Several people clapped, and during a chorus of oohs and aahs, the lights came back on.

Across the long table, where Tom had made sure Dallas was seated with him and his wife, Eric's eyes bored into hers as if the lights had never gone out. As if even in the dark he'd been drawn unerringly to her. And like a deer caught in the headlights, Dallas held his gaze, totally powerless to look away.

"This is rich. This is just too friggin' rich," Tom murmured, drawing her attention. "I should have brought a damn camera."

Thankfully the waiters began serving the Baked Alaska, and Dallas used the distraction to pull herself together. If she were smart, she'd excuse herself from the table and leave the party. Between his staring and the other guests' curiosity, she was bound to trip up. Make a fool of herself.

She'd purposely come after dinner so that she could flit about the room just out of his reach, engage in some harmless flirting, make him a little crazy and then disappear. The last thing she'd wanted was to be stuck at the table. Damn, she didn't even like Baked Alaska.

Her gaze drew back to him. Sitting beside him, a slim fortyish woman wearing too many diamonds on her fingers and an unhealthy tan had managed to monopolize his attention. Dallas used the opportunity to give him a once-over. Watch the way his mouth quirked up on one side in a sort of lopsided smile.

He really was good-looking in a conservative way. She'd like to see his hair a little longer, but that was cosmetic. The basics—the structural stuff, like the strong square chin—were there. Great lips, too. Nice and full on the bottom.

Then again, the clean-cut look wasn't bad for a change. Many of the guys she worked with had hair long enough to tie into a ponytail. Except for her best bud Tony, and even his dark, shaggy mop rested on his collar.

Tom made an odd gurgling noise behind his napkin, trying to stifle a laugh. "Look at him. He's in a daze talking to Miriam Lancaster. Doesn't even know what hit him. Did you see when he was trying to get my attention earlier? Do I have a poker face, or what?"

"Tom, stop it." Serena's warning voice was low, but both Dallas and the woman next to her heard. Serena's voice dropped a few pitches. "Besides making an ass out of yourself, you're going to blow it."

"Okay, okay." He stared at his plate until he was able to compose himself. It lasted three seconds before he started to chuckle again. "Did you see his face when—?"

"Tom, I mean it. I'll leave." Serena glanced at Dallas. "This is so incredibly juvenile. I'm sorry he involved you."

"Juvenile, hell. This is priceless." Tom's eyes gleamed until Serena picked the linen napkin off her lap and started to fold it, preparing to get up. "All right, I'll shut up."

She hesitated and then laid the napkin back down on her lap. Tom cast another glance at Eric and then at Dallas, pressed his lips together and picked up his fork.

Through the rest of dessert, Dallas sat quietly even though her heart raced like a thoroughbred rushing for the finish line. She'd figured she'd be nervous. And she was a little. Had almost backed out at the last minute. She'd certainly never expected the exhilaration she felt or the giddy headiness of power and control that continued to build.

While Eric knew nothing about her, she knew a lot about him. Knew he was a Columbia graduate who'd been steadily climbing the ladder of success from the day after he'd graduated. His hard work had paid off, and he was a rising star with Webber and Thornton, a company that believed in family and socializing outside of the office. Eric was the only holdout, unmarried and never even bringing a date to the company functions.

She liked that about him. A rebel, kind of like herself. But the similarity ended there. His friends and acquaintances belonged to an elite circle. The kind she shunned. No, not shunned, really. That wasn't accurate. But her world was definitely more eclectic. By choice.

But that's what made tonight's cameo appearance fun. No one knew anything about her. Not even Tom. He assumed she was a freelance model. She hadn't bothered to correct him. Wouldn't he be surprised if he discovered the truth?

She surveyed the other guests, all dressed to the nines, every hair in place, perfect manicures and polite smiles. They'd all be surprised to learn what she really did for a living. Disgusted maybe. As her parents were. To some extent, at least her brother and sister understood her need for autonomy. Not that they approved of her choices.

Dessert seemed to go on forever. Lots of cognac and fancy liqueurs were served. Fortunately enough subdued chatter muffled private conversations that she was able to easily fend off the polite curiosity of the other guests before Eric could get wind of their exchange.

According to Tom, only he, Serena and Mrs. Webber knew about the joke. Everyone else thought she was a visiting friend of the Webbers' absent daughter. Dallas stuck to the story, and curiosity generally died quickly.

Not Eric's, though. His gaze often strayed in her direction, although to his credit, the woman beside him would never know he was distracted. He smiled and inclined his head toward her when she spoke, did all the courteous things expected of him.

Only Dallas knew his thoughts were about her, that more than curiosity burned in his eyes when they met hers. Every nerve ending in her body reacted. As if two live wires connected and sparked with each look.

She tried to avoid the contact. Pretended interest in a boring conversation with Serena about the upcoming Heart Ball and the local celebrities who'd be attending. But she was just as hopeless, her gaze drawing back to him, admiring the breadth of his shoulders, the generosity of his smile, as the woman kept him busy.

He looked at her suddenly as if he'd felt the weight of her stare. To her amazement, she didn't look guiltily away. She held his gaze for a long, torturous moment, gave him a slow smile that invited all sorts of possibilities.

He wasn't shy about returning the volley. His gaze wandered down the front of her dress, lingering just long enough on her breasts to remain respectful yet make her tingle all the way down to her toes.

She finally had to look away. Or end up in an embarrassing puddle on the floor. He had the most incredibly intense eyes. The eyes of a man who knew what he wanted and went after it with everything he had in his arsenal. The thought frightened her, fascinated her, and then she remembered that she had the power here. Anything that happened would be by her design. She was no Cinderella hoping to be swept off her feet, rescued from life's drudgery.

Dallas's life was just fine, with or without a man. Less reliance on the old vibrator might be nice for a change, but that didn't mean she was willing to settle for just anyone. But Eric…well, he was looking like a pretty damn good substitute. Smart, attractive, successful, ambitious. Not that his view of success was important to her. In fact, her lack of interest in such matters was what put her at odds with her family.

But all that along with his standing in the business community made him a safe bet. At least for a couple of nights. What would it hurt? He didn't even know who she was. Even if he tried to contact her through the store, Trudie was the only one who knew her and Trudie wouldn't tell him anything. Trudie thought she was insane for doing this as it was.

Maybe she was crazy. This certainly wasn't her style. Her gaze drew to Eric again. He'd been watching her. Her pulse skidded. She nearly dropped her fork. This was going to be one hell of a night.

HE HAD TO TALK TO HER AGAIN. Alone. Away from the party. The Baked Alaska dishes had been cleared from the table. Cognac had been served. People had begun milling around. In about a half an hour they would start leaving. He had to make his move.

If he could find her. She'd left the table five minutes ago. He'd tried to follow but gotten waylaid by Brian Sutter's wife. Brian motioned for her a moment later, but Eric couldn't get away before Eve Dinton ambushed him.

Tonight of all nights it seemed as if everyone had to talk to him. Normally he didn't mind making polite conversation with his coworkers' wives, but if he heard about another unfair Little League game or about the rising cost of produce, he'd jump off the...

"Hello again."

Her feminine scent tickled his senses even before he turned to find her directly behind him. His attention immediately went to her glistening peach-tinted lips. They parted slightly and she drew back a step.

"I'm sorry. I didn't mean to intrude," she said almost in a whisper, and he realized he was just standing there. Staring. Speechless. Like an idiot.

"You didn't." He touched her arm when it looked as if she might take off. "Not at all."

She smiled tentatively. "You seemed so deep in thought."

"The truth is—" he lowered his voice "—I was thinking about the Webbers' rooftop garden."

"Oh." Her eyebrows drew together, and she hesitated, looking confused. "You like to garden?"

He laughed. "I was thinking about jumping off."

Her eyes widened.

"This isn't exactly my first choice for spending an evening."

"Ah, I see."

"Nice people." He shrugged. "But I see most of them every day at the office."

"Coworkers are kind of like family. You don't choose them," she said thoughtfully. "But you do have to make nice whether you like them or not."

He snorted. "That's debatable."

She smiled. "You get a point for honesty."

"Does that mean you'll go someplace for a drink with me?"

"Leave here?"

"I know this bar right around the corner. It's a nice place with piano music and—"

She'd started shaking her head. "I can't."

"Okay," he said slowly, "no problem."

"I'd like to. really…"

"But?"

She glanced over at Tom and Serena still sitting at the table. "I just don't think I should leave."

"Tell you what, how about we take a couple of cognacs up to the garden?"

"On the roof?"

"Sure. It's quiet. Great view of Central Park and Columbus Circle."

She seemed reluctant though definitely interested. "Won't the Webbers mind?"

"Not a bit."

"Sounds like you've done this before."

He smiled. "Actually I've only been up there once, when Mrs. Webber gave the grand tour a couple of years ago."

She glanced at her watch. "I suppose it would be all right for a few minutes."

"Then you turn into a pumpkin?"

Her lips curved in a mysterious smile. "Something like that."

THE GARDEN AREA WASN'T LARGE. Dimly lit, about the size of a guest room, flowers grew everywhere. Red geraniums, white daisies and sprays of pink blossoms spilled from several barrel-size stone urns. A trellis leaning against the reddish brick was covered with tiny climbing white roses that perfumed the air with their seductive scent.

Beyond the decorative black wrought iron that surrounded the rooftop garden were the lights of Manhattan and the shadows of Central Park.

"What a fantastic view." Hands gripping the rail, she leaned out, a gentle breeze blowing back her honeyblond hair, giving him an unobstructed view of her profile. The small, slightly upturned nose and skin that was remarkably flawless except for the scar.

Eric's curiosity got the better of him and he asked, "How did you get that?"

She turned to look at him and he pointed to his own chin. Her hand shot up to touch the marked area, her mouth twisting wryly.

She rolled her eyes. "Totally my fault. I got it at work when I wasn't paying attention."

"At work? How?"

She looked away. "This is a beautiful view. I wonder how much one of these co-ops cost." She smiled. "Not that I'd ever be able to afford one."

"I will someday."

Her eyebrows rose. "Ambitious or optimistic?"

He laughed. "Both."

"I wish you luck." She gave him a peculiar smile and then turned away to look out over Central Park.

"You must make good money modeling."

A smile played at the corners of her mouth. "What makes you think I'm a model?"

He stared, waiting for a telltale flicker to cross her face. She didn't even blink. "Aren't you?"

"No. But I'm flattered." She seemed so damned sincere. Maybe he was going crazy.

"Then what do you do?"

"Why?"

He shrugged. "Just making conversation."

"Then you won't mind talking about something else." Her lips curved in a smile that made him her slave.

A totally new experience for him. He liked women, of course, but he hadn't found one yet that had him thinking with the wrong head. Not since high school, anyway. "You like being the mystery woman, huh?"

The smile lingering on her lips, she lifted her chin and shook back her hair, lifting her face to the balmy breeze.

"So, if I can't get more than your name, how am I going to ask you out to dinner?"

After a moment's hesitation she looked directly at him and asked, "When?"

"Tomorrow night." God, he hoped he could get a reservation this late. "Amuse Bouche. It's that new restaurant at the—"

"I know it." Amusement lit her eyes. "Trying to impress me?"

"Damn right."

She laughed. "Another point for honesty. But unless you had another date cancel on you, we will not be getting into Amuse Bouche tomorrow night."

"I confess. No reservations, but I know the maître d'."

"Ever been to Hakata on West Forty-eighth?"

He frowned. "Sushi place, isn't it?"

"Among other things."

Just his luck, the woman was one of those adventurous-eater types. That was the trouble with New Yorkers. They weren't happy with a simple steak. "You wanna go there?"

She grinned. "Ever tried sushi?"

He sighed. All the guys in the office kidded him. When they went for sushi, he went to McDonald's. "I have a feeling I'm about to."

"Your enthusiasm is overwhelming."

"The stuff is raw. Can't be good for you."

She laughed. "Common misconception. Sushi can include raw fish but not necessarily. Don't worry. I'm a pro at ordering for neophytes. I'll be gentle with you."

He cleared his throat and tried not to make anything of the way she moistened her lips. Tried not to stare at her glistening lower lip. "Not too gentle. That would take out all the excitement."

Her eyebrows rose.

Eric smiled. "Bring it on."

She laughed, deep and throaty, and the sound skated down his spine. "You're giving me carte blanche?"

"I'm all yours." He hoped they weren't talking about sushi. Or he was screwed.

"Hmm…"

He moved closer. She didn't retreat. Excellent sign. "So, what would you like to do with me?"

"Oh, I never tip my hand too soon."

"Oh, right. A woman of mystery and surprise."

"You have no idea."

"I'm willing to stick around until I get an idea."

She smiled. "You get another point for being adventurous."

"Yeah? And what exactly are these points worth?"

She tilted her head to the side and pursed those sexy lips of hers. "I'll have to think about it."

"I don't." He took her hand, and when she didn't resist, he pulled her against him and slid his arms around her narrow waist.

She tilted her head back, her eyes glittering with unmistakable challenge. He lowered his head and she lifted her chin to meet his lips. They touched, gently at first, tentative, searching, exploring, and then she opened her mouth to him.

He slid his tongue between her lips and tasted her eagerness. That's all the permission he needed to plunge deeper. When she put her hands on his chest and slid her palms up to his shoulders, the tips of her fingers doing this little stroking thing that drove him crazy, he stifled a moan, willed his sudden hard-on to calm down before he scared the hell out of her.

But he couldn't calm down and she didn't scare. Instead she moved her hips, taunting him, driving him beyond insane. He cupped her backside, not sure if he wanted to stop her or make her grind harder.

Taking the decision out of his hands, abruptly she moved back, stared at him for a moment and then let her hands slide down his chest. "I have to go."

"Now?"

She smiled. "Tomorrow?"

"Yeah, sure— Wait!"

She'd already headed for the door that led to the stairs but stopped hesitantly and then turned to him.

"Dallas?"

"I'll be there at seven," she said and then took off.

4

DALLAS HAD BARELY FINISHED her first cup of coffee when Wendy plodded into the kitchen, still wearing red boxers and a white tank top—her preferred pajamas.

"What are you doing up so early?" Dallas asked, wondering the same thing about herself. She'd only had four hours' sleep, tops. After she'd gotten home, she'd been so wired, she'd stayed up and watched *Pretty Woman* for the twentieth time.

Well, she hadn't actually watched it. Stared, really. While she'd replayed the kiss over and over again in her head. While she'd imagined his hands curving over her butt, drawing her against his erection.

"I'm dying to hear about last night." Wendy got her usual morning cola out of the fridge. "Did he totally freak when he saw you?"

Dallas smiled, thinking about the stunned look on his face as he'd approached her. "He pretty much kept his act together when we were introduced. Although I'm not sure when he first spotted me."

"Who did he think you were?" She popped the tab of the can, sat cross-legged on the love seat and then yawned before taking her first sip.

"A friend of his boss's daughter. But we kept it vague."

"How late were you out?"

"I got in around midnight. You need a haircut."

Wendy's hand went to her spiky hair, and she hopelessly tried to pat it down. "I know. As soon as I get a few bucks together, I will. Maybe next Friday."

Dallas forced herself to keep her mouth shut. She was always ready to bail someone out. It wasn't that she was a pushover. She preferred to think of herself as a nurturer. Anyway, even if she offered Wendy a loan, she wouldn't take it. To her credit, Wendy watched her finances. "Any news on the audition?"

"I didn't make the final cut."

"I'm sorry."

"*C'est la vie.*" Wendy shrugged. "Maybe I should start sleeping with directors."

"Right." Dallas rolled her eyes. "That would be a good move."

"Hey, I didn't get up early to talk about how I screwed up yet another audition. Tell me about last night."

Dallas briefly turned away to pour another cup of strong black coffee. "Speaking of getting up early, I had to walk Bruiser again."

"Oh, no. Sorry. You should have knocked on my door."

"He yelped and howled for five minutes. If he couldn't get you up, I doubt I could have."

Wendy sighed, and then her lips started to curve as the ugly black mutt, having heard his name, lumbered ... shioned basket and then stretched before leaping up onto the love seat with Wendy. "He's so cute, isn't he?"

"Adorable. Especially at six in the morning."

Wendy gave her a sheepish look but then narrowed her eyes. "You're trying to avoid talking about last night."

Dallas rubbed the back of her neck. "Not really," she said, even as she privately acknowledged there was some truth there. "Last night was great. More fun than I'd expected."

"Yeah?"

"Yeah." Dallas leaned with her elbows on the kitchen counter that served as their table and a room divider. She cradled her mug in her hands and stared at the black liquid. "Eric is really a nice guy."

"And?"

"And I'm seeing him again tonight."

Wendy's hand froze in Bruiser's curly black fur. "You're kidding."

"Why not?"

"Alone?"

"At a restaurant. I'm not totally insane."

"This is so totally not you."

"That's the fun part." Dallas grinned. "It's not me."

Wendy put down her cola, linked her fingers together as she often did when she angsted over something, which wasn't often enough. She generally acted first, thought later. "Okay, what's really going on here?"

"Nothing." Dallas straightened, her defenses rising. "What's with you?"

"You're worrying me."

"This coming from someone who'd sleep with a director for a role?" Dallas snorted. "Besides, you're the one who encouraged me to go last night."

"Hey, I was kidding about the director." Wendy rubbed her eyes and sighed heavily. "How much did you tell this guy about yourself?"

"I haven't told him anything."

"Nothing?"

"Nothing."

Wendy studied her with an annoying mixture of curiosity and concern. "You don't trust him enough to tell him anything about yourself but you're willing to date him."

"It's not about trust. And I'm not dating him. It's one time. Jeez." Dallas sipped her coffee and took a mental time-out.

"I don't like the idea of you seeing him alone."

"We won't be alone, *Mom*. That's why I chose a restaurant."

"Which one?"

"Like I'm going to tell you."

"Why not?"

"I don't want you spying on me."

"Would I do something like that?"

In a New York minute. Dallas didn't bother to answer. Only gave her a look.

"Okay, what if I promise not to?"

"What does it matter which restaurant?"

"If he turns out to be a serial killer and no one ever sees you again, I need something to tell the police."

Dallas groaned. "He's not a serial killer. He works for Webber and Thornton Advertising, for goodness' sakes. If anything, he's too conservative for me."

"Really?" Wendy smiled. "So, why are you going tonight?"

Dallas stared blankly at her friend. The truth was she had no idea.

SHE'D LIED. TO WENDY AND to herself. As soon as she saw him, Dallas knew why she'd agreed to come. She wanted him. Even for just one night. The situation presented the perfect opportunity. Anonymous sex. Behavior she normally wasn't into. But something about him really drew her. Sparked a need she'd suppressed for a long time.

He stood near the register, stoically watching the guys making sushi behind the bar. He'd beaten her to the restaurant. And she was five minutes early.

After spending more time deciding what to wear than she'd care to admit, she'd chosen her newest pair of low-riding jeans and a light blue stretchy top that exposed about an inch and a half of her midriff and showed off her new tan, courtesy of Trudie. Casual but not sloppy.

Eric had dressed up a little more, in khakis and a hunter-green designer polo shirt, his tasseled loafers perfectly polished. She glanced down at her sequined flip-flops. At least her toes were polished; an electric pink, again courtesy of Trudie.

His fascinated interest in the sushi-making process came to an abrupt halt and he took a step back. The chef presented a plate of intimidating *hamachi*-and-eel sushi he'd been working on to a couple at the bar. Dallas smiled, and taking pity on Eric, she moved toward him.

"Hi."

He turned to her with relief in his eyes. "You showed up."

"Of course. I suggested the place, remember?"

He half smiled, and she realized he wasn't talking about the sushi.

The petite Japanese hostess returned from seating another couple and grabbed two menus off the counter. "How many?" she asked without a trace of an accent.

"Two," Dallas said, "and we'd prefer a table in the back if you have one."

"Let's see…"

While the woman searched the crowded restaurant, Eric whispered, "We can still make a break. There's a steak house right around the corner."

Dallas laughed. "Behave yourself and I won't make you eat anything raw."

"Follow me, please." The woman led them toward the back, her waist-long black hair swaying and shimmering like expensive silk as she wove in between tables. "Is this all right?" she asked, waving a perfectly manicured hand with long red fingernails at a table for two in the far corner.

"Perfect." Eric flashed her a grin that put a sparkle in her dark eyes.

"Enjoy your meal." She left the menus on the table and moved back toward the front as if she were gliding on air.

Dallas sighed as she took her seat. She really didn't mind being so tall, liked it usually, but sometimes she envied the seemingly effortless femininity of petite women.

Eric sat, too, his back toward the other diners. He didn't pick up his menu, only stared at her. Not in a rude way but enough to make her uneasy.

She cleared her throat. "Do you trust me to order for you?"

"Is this where the 'I'll be gentle' part comes in?"

"I thought you didn't like gentle."

"Depends."

"On what?"

His lips curved as he thoughtfully studied her for a moment. "So, that's how you wanna play."

She smiled back. "I'm not playing."

Challenge flickered in his eyes, but before he could deliver a comeback, the waitress appeared for their drink orders. He asked for a scotch, and Dallas ordered white wine. But that would be it for her. Work started at seven tomorrow.

"You come here often?" he asked, glancing around at the other diners, mostly tourists, mostly couples but a few families.

"This is only the third time, but the food is good and reasonable considering they advertise in one of those tourist magazines." She stopped herself from volunteering that it was also close to her apartment.

"Yeah, I was surprised you chose a tourists' hangout. I figured you must live nearby."

She smiled and picked up the menu even though she

knew exactly what she'd order. "You'd better have a look at the menu."

"I already know what I want."

The huskiness in his tone made her look up. She met his eyes and there was little doubt as to what he meant. She held his gaze but only for a moment before she had to look away. He didn't scare her. She frightened herself. Never before had the reckless urge to shun common sense been so strong. To jump in headfirst and consider the consequences later.

What the hell was it about him that made her want to be foolish? She pretended to study the menu, hoping her ridiculous desire to skip dinner and go straight to a hotel room would pass.

"What are you going to have?" she asked, keeping her eyes lowered to the menu.

"The teriyaki rib eye steak."

"You big chicken," she said, shaking her head at him.

"Hey, it's not like I'd ask them to leave off the teriyaki sauce."

They both laughed.

She laid down the menu. "How adventurous of you."

"You have no idea."

"Where are you from?"

"The Pittsburgh area. And you?"

She'd expected the return question and saw no harm in answering. "Right here. I was born at New York General, although I grew up mostly in Tarrytown. It's about forty minutes away."

"I know the area. Nice."

She nodded. "So green and pretty. I miss it but I like living in the city."

"Which part is that?"

She smiled. "How long have you lived here?"

"In Manhattan, about five years." His gaze roamed her face, lingered on her mouth. "I think our drinks are coming. Ready to order dinner?"

"Are you in a hurry?"

He gave her that sexy look again. "As a matter of fact, I am."

THEY LEFT THE RESTAURANT AN hour later. The sun had set, but there was still another half hour of light left. No way would Eric let this evening end. He still didn't know her last name or anything else about her. Other than she was from Tarrytown but now lived in the city.

Of course, knowing she'd grown up in Tarrytown provided more insight. He could safely bet his Rolex that her family had some money. The upper-middle-class community was a far cry from the steel-mill neighborhood where he'd grown up. Hell, even the Rockefellers had an estate there.

Although he didn't need particulars to know she came from a genteel background. Breeding showed in every step she took. The softness in her voice. The graceful way she moved. Modeling, of course, gave her polish, but she had her own natural panache that couldn't be learned or faked.

"How about a walk?" he asked before she could flag a cab and disappear.

"Sure. It's nice out. Not as sticky as last week."

"I say we head for Central Park."

Her eyebrows rose. "It'll start getting dark by the time we get there."

"Afraid of the big bad wolf?"

"Should I be?"

He smiled. "I think Tom probably assured you that I'm an okay guy."

"Tom?"

He shoved his hands in his pockets as they turned down Sixth Avenue. He badly wanted to touch her, but he'd wait for a signal. Let her call the shots. That's what she wanted. That's why she insisted on the secrecy.

"Was Tom at the party?" She seemed genuinely confused, which gave him pause.

"I figured it out, Dallas. We both saw you in the display window. Tom had to have put you up to this."

"What are you talking about?" She slid him a sidelong glance, her eyebrows drawn together in a skeptical frown.

"There's no other explanation."

She shook her head with a wry smile. "Maybe we ought to skip the walk. You need some serious rest."

"Yeah, I hardly slept last night." He kept watching her, noticed her near misstep, the way her cheeks colored a little. "What about you?"

"Fine. I slept just fine."

"Good. Then you shouldn't be in any hurry to get home."

She laughed. "Very sly."

"Look out." He grabbed her arm and pulled her close when she nearly collided with a shabbily dressed man staggering wildly, obviously drunk.

"Thanks." She leaned against Eric as she glanced over her shoulder at the man, who'd already passed by—but not so his rank odor. "Sad, isn't it?"

The compassion in her eyes touched him, as misplaced as it was. He took another look at the guy, evidently homeless and drunk. "He needs a good meal instead of spending his money on booze."

"You don't know his circumstances." She pulled away. "He may have just lost his job or received some horrible news."

"You're right." He drew her back against him and slipped an arm around her shoulders. "I shouldn't have said that. But there were a lot of steel mills where I grew up. I saw what happened to men who lost their jobs."

Looking away, she murmured, "Yeah, I've seen it, too."

That surprised him. What did she understand about that world? About the blue-collar laborer who was so readily sacrificed to improve the bottom line of a corporation's financial statement? He understood. Too well. His brothers were fools for languishing in the mills, and settling for the same scraps their father had.

He caught a glimpse of Central Park a couple of blocks away, along with the lineup of carriages and horses with their colorful hats. "I have an idea. How about a carriage ride?"

"Are you serious?" She laughed softly. "Only tourists do that."

"Correct me if I'm wrong, but didn't we just eat in a touristy restaurant?"

"Touché."

"Come on. Let's pick out a horse."

She made a face. "We don't have much time before it gets dark."

He smiled, his body thrumming with anticipation. "Sometimes interesting things happen in the dark."

5

BY THE TIME THEY GOT TO THE fourth horse—wearing a straw hat with an orange band and large drooping yellow daisies—Dallas knew Penelope was the one for them. The chestnut-colored mare had sweet, soulful eyes and a soft neigh, and Dallas immediately bonded with her.

She stroked her velvety head. "Penelope's definitely the one."

"You're sure now?"

"Positive." Glancing at Eric, she realized he was teasing her and she lightly punched him in the arm.

"Okay." He laughed. "Penelope it is."

He spoke to the driver a moment—an older man with drooping eyes and a face lined and brown as shoe leather—and then helped Dallas into the carriage. In seconds they were trotting into the park, the sound of Penelope's clopping hooves on the asphalt stirring a wistfulness in Dallas.

She sighed. "I haven't ridden in ages. I used to ride every weekend when I was in high school."

"Where?"

"At my grandparents'. They had a couple of Arabians and a palomino."

"Am I allowed to ask where?"

She smiled. "In Connecticut."

He slid his arm around the back of the seat and she snuggled closer. "They have ranches in Connecticut?"

"I didn't say they owned a ranch."

"Just recreational stables."

"You ask too many questions."

"I believe that was a statement."

She just shook her head. He chuckled, and then they rode in silence for a while, enjoying the slight breeze produced by the movement of the carriage.

Ironically, more and more questions about him paraded through her head. Based on what Tom had told her, she'd figured she knew exactly who Eric was. The Rolex around his wrist, the Gucci shoes, the designer clothes—all accessories of an image-conscious social climber—confirmed her belief.

Eric was exactly the kind of man her parents wished she'd bring home. He was precisely the type she never would.

But his comments about the steel mill usurped her logic. Made her wonder about his link to the other side of the coin. Not just because he had lived in an industrial city like Pittsburgh. A variety of jobs existed there just as in any other city. But there had been something personal in his voice, a tinge of bitterness that came from firsthand experience.

"See? Playing tourist isn't so bad, is it?" he whispered, his mouth so close to her ear that his warm breath sent a shiver down her spine.

"I'll admit this is nice." She turned her head toward him, knowing exactly what would happen.

His lips brushed hers lightly, a teasing swipe that left her wanting more. She angled toward him, resting her palm on his thigh. She heard his sharp intake of breath and realized just how high up she'd placed her hand. Resisting the urge to jerk back, she pressed her lips harder against his.

He ran the tip of his tongue across the seam of her lips until she opened to him. She heard voices along the path, someone giggling, but she didn't care. Her pulse raced with every swipe he took with his tongue, exploring the fleshy inside of her mouth, leisurely tracing her teeth.

Heat spread through her chest and up her neck. And then the warmth flooded her belly, spiraled lower, until she had to squeeze her thighs together.

Eric moved his hand to her waist, his fingers probing her bare skin where her shirt ended. She sucked in a breath as he explored her belly and then moved his hand higher so that he cupped the underside of her breast.

The driver started to whistle an unfamiliar tune. He hadn't turned around and seen them, she was relatively certain, but the reminder that they were out in public put a damper on her excitement.

Eric obviously sensed her retreat and stilled his hand. He broke the kiss and pulled back to look at her. She couldn't see his face very well. It seemed to have gotten dark so quickly.

"Something wrong?" he asked, his fingers idly stroking her skin.

"Other than the fact that we're in the middle of Central Park acting like two hormonal teenagers, no." She snarled. "Nothing's wrong."

"It's too dusky. No one saw anything other than us kissing."

She shifted so that his hand fell away from her belly.

"Tell you what, let's use the blanket." He reached behind him and brought out the small stadium-style blanket that had been left on the seat.

"It's too warm for a blanket."

"Exactly." He shook it out. "So why else do you think the driver left it."

She laughed. "He did not."

"Ask him."

"Right."

He laid the blanket across their laps. "Trust me. We aren't the first couple to neck in Central Park."

"I've always had a problem with the term 'trust me.'"

The carriage ran over a small bump and she fell against him.

"Sorry, folks," the driver muttered half over his shoulder without turning around.

Eric slid both his arms around her and brought her back against his chest. "Isn't that more comfortable?"

"It would be if I could—" She gasped as his hands moved up to cup her breasts. She leaned her head back and he kissed the side of her neck.

He inhaled deeply and whispered, "You smell good." He kissed her neck again, trailing his tongue to the area just below her ear. "You taste good."

She turned her head so that their lips met and slipped a hand between his thighs. Something he clearly hadn't expected. But wasted no time in using to his advantage.

He shifted his hips, and her palm slid against his bulging fly. His hardness startled her. Excited her. Empowered her. She twisted toward him, deepening the kiss, letting him slide his hand underneath her shirt. He reached her bra and worked his fingers inside, gently stroking the sensitive flesh around her nipple.

With her free hand she clutched the blanket to her chest. Not just for privacy but because he was making her crazy. What was she doing? She'd only met him last night. This wasn't her style.

She breathed in deeply. This was her fantasy, she reminded herself. She wasn't hurting anyone. In fact, it had been a long time since she'd felt this good. Felt the uncontrollable burning in her belly. Felt like saying *screw everything* and dragging him down to the grass.

He took her nipple between his fingers and she whimpered softly. He smothered the sound with his mouth, delving in deep with his tongue until she couldn't breathe. Couldn't think. Couldn't feel anything but his heat searing her skin, the feverish desire in his touch.

Like a sound echoing in a distant cave, she heard voices murmuring, laughing. Momentarily disoriented, she shifted, let her head fall back against his shoulder.

Approaching them on the path was another couple, on foot, not so far away. Dallas moved away from him and tugged down her bra and shirt. The blanket still hid them from view, but the spell had been broken.

Eric didn't move. He continued to hold her, his warm breath dancing over the side of her neck and ear. Once the couple had passed, he whispered, "My apartment isn't far from here."

She bit her lip. God, it was tempting. Incredibly tempting. She liked him. The chemistry was certainly there. This is what she wanted. So, what held her back?

She did have to get up early tomorrow.

What a load of crap. Her reluctance was about the whole fantasy thing. It would end. No more mystery woman. He'd find out she was an ordinary woman, working in construction, trying to pay off her student loan.

The polished nails and perfect hair, the sensational tan, the nice clothes—none of it was really her. If he passed her on the street while she was working in her normal torn jeans or coveralls, her hair tied back in its usual messy ponytail, he wouldn't give her a second look.

But then again, he'd only find out if she told him.

Which she'd probably blurt out once they'd made love. Except it would only be sex. Very different. So maybe...

"Dallas?"

Lost in thought, she jerked at the sound of his voice.

"Look, I didn't mean to push you. It's okay."

"It's not that. Really."

He kissed her briefly on the lips. "On Wednesday night one of my clients is having a reception. I'd like you to go with me." He paused, watching her closely. "Unless you have to work Wednesday night."

She did everything in her power not to laugh. His fishing was so obvious. Fortunately the original model had recovered and was back to work. "I don't work nights. Where's the reception?"

"At an art gallery on the Upper East Side. They'll be serving champagne and hors d'oeuvres. We can go out to dinner afterward." He kissed the side of her jaw. "Anywhere you want. Say you'll come with me."

The carriage began to slow just as the driver said, "End of the line, folks. Hope you enjoyed the ride." He slowly turned and grinned at them. "For thirty bucks, I'll take you around again."

"No, thanks." Dallas straightened and made sure she was put together before dropping the blanket. "I really do have to get up early tomorrow," she said to Eric and started to climb down.

"Wait. Let me go first." He hopped down before she could protest and then grasped her around the waist and lowered her to the ground.

"Thank you," she murmured, stopping herself from informing him that she was perfectly capable of climbing down by herself. She wasn't normally treated so chivalrously. In fact, she made it a point to be one of the guys. As it was, they needed little ammunition to harass her and the only other woman on the crew.

Eric handed the driver a couple of bills. She resisted arguing over who should pay. They'd already gone that round in the restaurant.

It didn't matter that it was a Sunday night. Around Fifth Avenue and Fifty-ninth there were always people on the streets, mostly tourists, returning from Broadway or dinner or watching the street entertainers.

Not far from the corner a magician transfixed his audience with disappearing balls and trinkets, earning him delighted gasps and fistfuls of change dropped into his proffered top hat.

"I know a place that makes the best cappuccino." Eric raised his hand to hail a cab.

Dallas smiled. "I'll have to pass."

"It's only five minutes away."

"Sorry."

He muttered a mild curse. "I've screwed up."

"No, you haven't," she said, touching his hand. "Not at all."

He turned his hand over until their palms met and squeezed gently. "Am I going to see you again?"

She nodded just as a cab pulled alongside the curb.

"Will you go with me on Wednesday night?"

"Yes."

"I don't have your phone number." He opened the cab door and stood aside for her.

"I'll call you."

"What if I can't wait until Wednesday?"

She smiled. "You can take this cab. There's another one behind it."

One side of his mouth hiked up. "I don't suppose you'd let me ride with you to your place."

"I don't suppose I would." She leaned toward him for a kiss. A brief, friendly good-night kiss.

He wanted more and took it.

He tugged her forward and she came up against him, her still-sensitive breasts pressed to his chest. He cupped her nape, and as she opened her mouth to his demanding kiss, he held her steady while he got his fill.

The impatient cabbie muttered something about turning on the meter. The interruption saved her from ending up on the sidewalk in a boneless mess. She pulled away from Eric, her knees close to giving out, and crawled into the backseat, yanking the door closed behind her.

On the other side of the closed window, Eric smiled and then mouthed *Good night.*

The cab pulled away. She tried to wave. She didn't have the strength.

"Yo, Shea." Tony St. Angelo called from hands cupped around his mouth. "You ready for lunch?"

"Five more minutes," Dallas hollered back and then used her sleeve to wipe the sweat off her brow.

Today was way too hot to be working outdoors. But that was the breaks. Just part of the job. That's why she got paid the big bucks.

Right.

She adjusted her sunglasses and then dug for her bottle of water without letting go of the heavy Stop sign she'd been holding most of the damn morning. She hated traffic duty. With a passion. Even shoveling rocks and brick from a razed building was preferable. But this was a punishment she often received. For no other reason than being a woman working in a man's world.

Tony was one of the good guys. One of the pathetically few who didn't blame her for "taking a man's job away from him." He always waited to have lunch with her, though he was allowed to break at any time. The two traffic workers had the only formally scheduled breaks. She even had to get permission to go to the bathroom.

She waited for the radio message and then dutifully carried her sign to the middle of the road, bringing traffic to a halt and enduring angry honking until the back loader cleared the intersection. Then she radioed to her partner on the other end to resume traffic and waited for someone to come and relieve her for lunch. She pushed back the top of her glove and checked her watch. As usual her relief wasn't in any hurry.

In the beginning, with the exception of Tony and Sam—and Billy, when the other guys weren't around— the rest of them had treated her like a pariah, pulling seniority and giving her jobs that no one else wanted. They had made snide remarks, sometimes crude ones, under their breaths when no one but she could hear. Even so, after they'd clocked out for the day, half of the stupid bastards had hit on her at least once.

That had mostly changed after she'd made it clear she wouldn't put up with that ridiculous behavior. Of course there were two exceptions who insisted on acting like macho idiots, but they were easy to ignore.

What really got to her was that Nancy—the other woman on the crew—put up with their harassment. She accepted after-work drink offers even though she couldn't stand the guys. But she was a single mother with limited skills who desperately needed the job and felt she had to play nice no matter what.

Dallas, on the other hand, stuck around partly out of stubbornness but mostly because she didn't know what else to do with her life. Nothing really called to her; she had no passion. Not like her brother or sister who both lived and breathed the intricacies of the law, or her father, a well respected judge, whose views on education and child abuse had achieved national notoriety. Even her mother had made a name for herself in the science community. Dallas envied them their passion and focus. While in graduate school, after she'd become disgusted with modeling, she'd gone to a temporary agency for work. She'd quickly found she hated sitting in front of a computer all day. Adding columns of numbers hadn't turned out to be her thing either.

Then a new temp agency had mistakenly placed her on a construction site. To her amazement, she'd found she liked working outdoors. She no longer had to worry about every morsel she ate or what to wear, or how many mistakes she made typing. After she punched her time card, she didn't have to worry about anything related to work.

"Okay, Shea. Lunch." Rocky roughly grabbed the sign out of her hand. He was one of the two Neanderthals left and hated relieving her. "That's thirty minutes only. Got it?"

"Really?" She raised her eyebrows and looked at him over her sunglasses. "It hasn't changed?"

"Don't be a smart-ass," he mumbled and snatched the radio.

"I wouldn't want to take away your job." She smiled sweetly and walked away from his barrage of curses.

Tony was waiting for her at the curb with both of their lunch pails. "He giving you a bad time again?"

"What's new?"

"Damn low-life bottom-feeder. I still think you should report him."

"Like that would help." She took her *Aladdin* lunch pail—a gag gift from Wendy— from him and they both turned toward the small park they'd found last week. "He's in so tight with old man Capshaw, it's pathetic."

"Yeah, he's either kissing ass or sleeping with the old guy."

Dallas laughed. "You would think of that."

"Tell you what, how about I just punch him out in the meantime?"

"Hey, if that's what I wanted, I'd do it myself."

This time Tony laughed. "Yeah, you probably would. Seriously, though, I don't care how tight Rocky is with Capshaw, this is a legal issue. Capshaw's Construction is too big. He can't afford to ignore a complaint and get ripped apart by the EEO, ERA or whoever the hell is involved."

"You're right. But I don't think that's enough. One complaint would only get a wrist slapping."

"Both you and Nancy need to—"

"You're preaching to the choir."

"Yeah, I know. It just pisses me off that you have to put up with so much crap when you do a better job than half those losers." They'd sat under a tree and he opened his lunch pail. "Shit, peanut butter and jelly again."

Dallas shook her head as she removed her gloves, and

then brought out her cheese and crackers and fruit. "Tony, you aren't married. You made your own lunch."

"Yeah, I know." He gave her that wide grin that had surely broken many hearts. "I haven't grocery shopped in a while."

She took off her baseball cap, tightened her ponytail, replaced the cap and then got out the hand sanitizer. "Why haven't you gotten married?"

"I've been saving myself for you. Wanna cola? I have an extra one."

"Come on. I'm serious."

"And nosy."

"Yeah, so," she said, laughing as she took the cola he offered.

He shrugged a shoulder. "Hell, I'm only thirty-one. I've got time."

"Here." She gave him a hunk of her Gouda.

"What about you?" he asked, his dark eyes suddenly full of curiosity. "Every time we go for a drink after work, you turn every guy's head in the bar. But you don't even talk about dating anyone."

"I keep waiting for you to ask."

He stared, speechless.

"I'm kidding." She winked. "You're my only friend here. I don't want to ruin a good thing."

"Yeah, that's what I'm thinking." He checked his watch and then bit into his sandwich.

She watched him chew, studying the clean lines of his jaw, the straight, almost patrician nose. His dark wavy hair was pulled back in a short ponytail. He was a really good-looking guy. The way his muscled biceps strained against his T-shirt sleeves caught the attention of nearly every woman who walked by.

But Dallas had never felt anything other than camaraderie with him. She had no idea why. Just no chemistry. No sparks like she had with Eric.

Just thinking about him made her all tingly inside.

How was she going to stand not seeing him until Wednesday night? That was almost forty-eight hours from now. Tomorrow night she had her meeting. Since she was the organizer, she damn well had better show up. Anyway, she had to get a dress for the reception on Wednesday night.

Thoughtfully she took a sip of cola. Tonight she wasn't doing anything. Her heart started to race as she summoned her courage. What the hell? She didn't have anything to lose. She was the mystery woman.

She checked her watch. Eight minutes left.

"Hey, Tony, I've got to make a phone call," she said as she started to gather her stuff. "You want the rest of this cheese and crackers?"

"You talkin' to me?" He grinned at his lousy imitation. "Leave everything. I'll pick it up. Go."

She smiled her thanks. Her cell phone already out of her pocket.

6

ERIC GOT HIMSELF A SOFT drink out of the refrigerator in the coffee room. The pastrami sandwich he'd ordered from the corner deli would be here any minute. On the few occasions he'd ordered lunch in, they'd delivered promptly.

Never in his life had he waited for a woman to call. Not even in high school when he'd had the hots for Tammy McIntosh, who'd had the best breasts east of the Mississippi and had given him his first and thankfully only hickey. Every guy in school had wanted to take her out, and he'd had the pleasure three or four times. When things had started to cool between them, he'd moved on. No waiting around by the phone for him.

But today he waited. Even skipped going out to lunch with Tom just in case Dallas called. Tom hadn't volunteered squat about Saturday night. Which was really ticking Eric off. His so-called friend's innocent act had gotten real old. That's why Eric hadn't told him about dinner last night. Screw him.

On his way down the hall back to his office, he heard the delivery kid at the reception desk. He'd already left money with the receptionist so he needed only to grab the bag on his way back to his office.

"You had a call," his secretary said as he approached his office.

"What? Who?" Damn it. He'd been gone less than two minutes.

Looking confused and curious, Lucy handed him the pink message slip. "A woman. She said you'd understand."

"I told you to page me if I had any calls."

Lucy shrugged. "She wouldn't wait."

He frowned at the message. And then he smiled. It read: *Tonight. By the magician. Six-thirty. Dallas.*

"What's this?"

At the sound of Tom's voice behind him, Eric pocketed the message. "None of your business."

Lucy's eyes widened.

Tom laughed. "Testy today, aren't we?"

Eric sighed and went into his office.

Tom followed. "Is that your secret meeting place? By the magician?"

Eric sat at his desk and glared at him. "You read my message?"

"Yeah, but just over your shoulder. I'm assuming this is the same woman from Saturday night."

Ignoring him, Eric set aside the ad campaign he'd been working on for his newest client. Ironically an upscale take-out sushi place. He opened the white paper sack and brought out his sandwich. Normally he'd give Tom the dill pickle. Screw him.

"Come on." Tom sat in the burgundy leather chair opposite Eric's desk. "What's going on?"

"You tell me."

"What are you talking about?" The corner of Tom's mouth twitched. He could barely contain a grin.

"I'm not stupid. I know you set up Saturday night."

Tom frowned, pretending confusion. "Saturday night? I don't get it."

Eric unwrapped his sandwich. Forget it. He didn't need Tom to admit his involvement. In fact, he probably should be thanking the pain in the ass. "Don't you have work to do?"

"Come on. Tell your buddy Tom what's going on."

Lucy briefly ducked her head in. "Tom, Mr. Webber is looking for you."

"Thanks." He got to his feet and, with an annoying grin, said, "Later," before he disappeared.

Eric leaned back in his chair and stared at his diploma and awards on the opposite wall. His office wasn't much to write home about. Fairly small, sparse, just like all the other offices except for Webber's and Thornton's corner suites. The money and attention had gone into the conference room, where the ad execs met with clients.

He forgot about his sandwich. Forgot about the new ad campaign. Forgot about Tom and his stupid antics. All he could think about was seeing Dallas tonight.

By the magician.

Interesting choice. She could have named a restaurant. Or any number of places. Why Central Park, near the magician? Of course, having had to leave a message probably had something to do with not getting specific. Or maybe…

His heart started to pound. Blood rushed straight to

his groin. He'd told her he didn't live far from there. Maybe she wanted to go to his place.

The thought took hold and wouldn't dissolve. He barely remembered eating his sandwich. But suddenly it was gone and he was crumpling up the wrapper.

The rest of the afternoon was a total loss. Flashes from last night haunted him. Consumed his concentration. He swore he could smell her honeyed scent, could feel the weight of her breasts in his palms. His body responded fiercely to the memory of her slipping her hand between his thighs. After that, he couldn't even get comfortable.

An hour earlier than usual he packed it up. He hadn't gotten a damn bit of work done for three hours. All he could think about was Dallas.

SHE LEFT THE PLAZA HOTEL, where she'd stopped for a drink with Trudie, five minutes before the appointed hour. Trudie thought Dallas was insane for carrying on this charade. But, of course, Trudie's idea of adventure was trying out a new grocery store.

This was perfectly harmless, Dallas assured herself. She knew she wasn't the type of woman he wanted. He wasn't her type either. Not that she had a type. She'd had a couple long-term relationships, including going steady with Steve O'Neil for three chaste years in high school. Every one of the guys had been different. With the exception of Steve, she'd been the one to break off the relationship. The truth was, she didn't know what she wanted.

But she hadn't lied to Eric about herself. She simply

hadn't told him anything. He knew all he needed to. Simple sex required no history, no promises.

Eric was already there. He was listening to a couple playing the sax and singing on the corner. Her pulse already starting to race, she slowed to watch him a moment, enjoying the way his jeans hugged his long, lean legs. He had on a black T-shirt this time, but she'd bet anything it had some kind of designer logo on it. That was okay. She was glad he'd dressed more casually than last night. In fact, what she had in mind didn't require clothes at all.

The song ended, and Eric threw some bills in the basket at the couple's feet, then stepped away from the crowd and turned in her direction. He spotted her and smiled.

The way her heart seemed to flip-flop was totally ridiculous. Amazingly foolish. But only because he had such a good body. Not muscular but kind of lean and wiry, like a long-distance runner.

"Hi." He took her hand and bent to kiss her briefly on the lips.

The familiarity surprised her, and she stiffened.

He released her hand. "Guess I shouldn't have done that."

"No. I mean, it's fine. Really." She shrugged a shoulder, feeling awkward suddenly. "You just took me by surprise."

"So did you. Thanks for calling."

"I wasn't sure you'd show up."

He reared his head back. "You gotta be kidding."

She smiled, her confidence returning. "You could have had a meeting or something."

"I would have canceled it."

"Just like that?"

"Uh-huh." He smiled, his gaze slowly taking in the clingy peach-colored V-neck top she'd borrowed from Wendy. Probably a tad too small for Dallas, but she loved the color. "You look great. I mean, really terrific."

"Thanks," she murmured, a little embarrassed by his obvious appreciation but also glad she'd splurged on a trendy new pair of white capris after work. Might as well show off her tan while it lasted.

He took her arm and they started walking. "You have anything in mind?"

She nearly missed a step and had to take a deep breath before she answered. "A drink maybe."

"How about some dinner?"

"Okay." She wasn't the least bit hungry. But she supposed dinner could be a start. "Have any place in mind?"

"Hmm…" He thought for a moment. "You like Chinese?"

"Love it. But this time it's my treat. Nonnegotiable."

He smiled. "There's a hole-in-the-wall five blocks from here. Great food. They even cook everything."

She laughed. "You were a good sport last night."

"I still think that California roll had something raw in it."

"See? You're still alive."

He stopped and stared at her. "You swore there was nothing raw in—"

She burst out laughing. "Teasing. Only teasing." She held up her hands. "I swear."

With phony gruffness he grabbed one of her hands and pulled her toward him. An older lady wearing a huge straw hat and walking a Chihuahua had to side-step them and she muttered a surprising oath about them blocking the sidewalk.

Eric apologized, though unable to lose the smile, then steered them off to the side. "I thought she was going to sic Bruno on us."

"Don't underestimate those little suckers. One of my college roommates had a Chihuahua. He had me cornered a couple of times."

They'd started down Fifty-ninth again, and he looked over at her. "Where did you go to school?"

She hesitated. "Cornell."

"Whoa. Nice. Scholarship?"

"Partial."

He nodded. "What was your major?"

Dallas stalled a moment. She really didn't want to get into this personal a conversation, but nor did she want to ruin the evening. "Let's just say that much to my parents' delight, I'm not working in the same field in which I studied."

"Which would be?"

She smiled. "Are we there yet?"

He gave her a speculative look and then decided to drop it. "Almost. Hungry?"

She nodded, which was a lie but she'd effectively changed the subject. "Hope they aren't too crowded."

He took a long time looking at his watch. "They probably will be." He looked at her as they stopped for a red light. "I usually take out."

She held his gaze. "Fine."

"My place okay?" he asked slowly.

"Sure."

His eyes seemed to bore into hers. "It's only a block from Chun's."

"Let's go." The light turned green and they hurried across the street with the few other pedestrians who hadn't ignored the stop signal.

Eric didn't say much for the next block, which made Dallas nervous. Although she hadn't volunteered much conversation either. Her thoughts kept straying to later. When they got to his place. Of course, nothing had to happen. They could just have dinner. Talk. Kiss a little.

Yeah, right.

She was getting damp just thinking about being alone with him. About the way he'd kissed her last night and how she'd felt the warm, gooey sensation down to her toes. About how he'd gently cradled her breasts.

Her breathing came so quickly that he even glanced over at her. "Are you okay?"

Heat climbed her neck. "Yeah, I'm fine. Really." Fortunately she spotted a sign for Chun's on the corner. "We're almost there."

"Yeah, that's it," he said with a final concerned look before taking her arm and ushering her to the door.

He hadn't been kidding. The place truly was a hole-in-the-wall. Really tiny, with only four tables, all taken, and a counter crowded with paper bags, presumably containing take-out orders. Several people waited in line as a young Asian woman efficiently yanked slips from the bags, called names and rang up bills at the cash register.

The aroma of onions and garlic and exotic spices permeated the air. This place was obviously the real deal and not a watered-down version to appease Western tastes.

Behind the counter an older man and woman worked side by side, stirring pots and tending a large grill against the far wall, speaking loudly to each other in Chinese. One of the customers got up from the table and went to the corner, where there were pitchers of water and iced tea and a bucket of ice. Sitting on a hot plate was a glass carafe of hot tea. He poured himself some and then returned to the table and his two companions.

Dallas smiled. She liked the place already. Kind of homey and friendly.

"I know it smells pretty bad, but I promise the food is terrific," Eric said as he took her hand and pushed his way inside.

"Are you kidding? I think it smells great."

The cashier looked up and smiled broadly.

"Eric." She glanced over her shoulder. "Mom, Dad, look who's here."

The short, graying man at the grill turned around. He spotted Eric and put down the long wooden chopsticks he was using, his big grin displaying a gold-capped tooth. "My friend, where have you been? I haven't seen you for three weeks, I think."

"Been busy working."

The man wiped his hands on his apron and gave Dallas a curious glance. "I see."

Unlike his daughter, who had no trace of an accent, the man's English was heavily coated with his native dialect. The sly look he gave Eric, however, was universal.

"This is my friend, Dallas. And this is Jimmy Chun, owner and chef of this wonderful establishment."

Jimmy chuckled. "He likes to use funny words," he said and gave his palm another swipe across his stained apron before extending his hand to Dallas.

"Uh, Jimmy, I think you can skip the formality," Eric said, one eyebrow lifted at his friend's slightly soiled hand.

"Pleased to meet you." Dallas readily accepted the man's hand. If Eric only knew what her hands went through on a daily basis. Even wearing gloves all the time at work didn't totally protect them.

Jimmy grinned, a flicker of approval in his eyes. "You are most welcome here."

Eric waved to the woman still cooking. "Jimmy's wife, Ruth."

She smiled and then said something to her husband in Chinese, her tone slightly brusque. Dallas could sure guess what was said, with all the people lined up for their orders. Two more guys came in after they did, and the phone had rung twice. The place was really hopping. The food had to be good.

"Maybe we should come back," she whispered to Eric.

Jimmy heard. "No, no, you come with me."

He pushed aside the low swinging gate that separated

the galleylike kitchen from the eating area and motioned for them to follow. Jimmy led them into a small kitchen where a young man wearing headphones and singing was dumping a huge pot of cooked rice into a wok heating on a stove.

Jimmy touched him on the shoulder and the man stopped singing, turned toward them, a sheepish smile twisting his lips.

The kitchen was crowded with a stainless-steel commercial refrigerator, a double sink and a small stove. Too small for a business, but that's all that would fit. There was barely enough room for all four of them to be in there. Nevertheless she was impressed with how spotless the kitchen was kept.

"You tell me what you want. Anything." Jimmy jabbed a thumb into his chest. "You tell Jimmy and I cook for you. You like some orange chicken? Garlic shrimp?"

Eric put a hand on the shorter man's shoulder. "I'll give you an order, but no rush. I'll pick it up later. You need to go help Ruth. You have a lot of customers out there."

Jimmy waved a dismissive hand. "I have so many customers because of you. They can wait." With his hands motioning wildly, he barked instructions in Chinese to the young man.

"Jimmy, honestly we're not ready to eat. We have someplace to go." Eric briefly met her eyes and purposefully looked at his watch. "We'd like to pick up dinner in about an hour and a half, if that's okay."

"Anything for you, my friend." Jimmy looked at Dallas. "Something special for the lady? Our shrimp is very, very fresh today. Or how about some—"

"I love all kinds of food. Surprise us." She winked at Eric. "I hate to be rude, but we're going to be late."

"Right. I'll be back to pick up dinner in an hour and a half."

"You want us deliver?" Jimmy asked. "We deliver to you. One hour and a half."

"I'll call and let you know."

Grinning, Jimmy nodded. "Anything for my friend. You call."

"Thanks." Eric shook his hand. "Okay if we go out the back way?"

"Yes, yes. Please." He gestured toward the door.

Ruth called out something in Chinese, to which Jimmy responded in kind.

"See you later, Jimmy." Eric opened the door and motioned for Dallas to precede him.

"See you, my friend." Jimmy grinned with a raised hand and watched them go, seeming in no hurry to go back out and help his wife.

They ended up in a short alley with a foul odor thanks to the Dumpster stationed not more than four feet from the door and hurried to the street.

Eric made a face and muttered, "Sorry, who knew the place would be so jammed on a Monday."

"No problem." She shrugged. "We can eat anywhere. At the park if you like."

He gave her an odd look. "You're really something."

The appreciation warming in his eyes made her blush. "What?"

He kept staring at her, paying no attention to where they were walking, and then he said half under his breath, "You're going to be trouble, Dallas. Big trouble."

7

SHE WAS TRULY REMARKABLE. Eric thought about how Tom's wife, Serena, would have reacted to the whole Chun's experience. Or Ryan's wife or Grant's wife. All nice, attractive ladies, but they would have been totally freaked out to have been herded back into the kitchen and then led out to that putrid-smelling alley.

Hell, he couldn't even imagine Judy shaking Jimmy's not-so-sanitary hand. It wasn't that the women were snobs or anything, just more refined. Different tastes, different backgrounds. They weren't the type to eat in dives, no matter how good the food.

He glanced over at Dallas just as they approached his building. She put them all to shame. Not just the way she looked... God, as if that wasn't enough. His chest and groin tightened just looking at her in those tight white pants that looked like a second skin molding that perfect butt. Nice and round and firm. Made his palms itch to cup her to him. Feel her pearled breasts against his chest.

He forced himself to look away before his jeans got so damn tight his doorman would have to help him to the elevator. Anyway, it wasn't just about the way she looked that turned him on or that set her apart from the other women he knew. It was the way she carried herself with confidence and grace. And more. Much more. Something indefinable that only years of stellar breeding could have produced.

Maybe tonight she'd tell him about herself, about her family. His desire to know about her went beyond curiosity. She fascinated him, occupied his thoughts more than was healthy for him or his career.

He stopped when they got to his apartment building and greeted the new doorman who'd started last week, after Hector had retired and moved to Miami. Eric gestured for her to enter the lobby.

She blinked at him in surprise. "You live here?"

Nodding, he led her to the elevator.

"Nice."

He smiled. "Too bad the lobby's bigger than my entire apartment."

"So is mine, but at least you have a doorman and an elevator."

"You have a walk-up?"

"It is now. The elevator broke and they won't repair it."

"Wow!" He frowned at her. Surely she could afford something better.

"Why are you surprised? It's great exercise. And certainly more affordable."

The elevator door opened, they both stepped inside and he punched the button for the fifth floor. "But having a doorman is more secure."

"True, but fortunately we haven't had any problems."

"We?"

She looked hesitant and his heart plummeted. "I have a roommate."

"Ah." He waited for her to drop the bomb.

"Her name's Wendy."

"Oh." He didn't even bother to hide his relief.

"Did you think—" She squinted at him. "I wouldn't be here with you if I were living with someone or— heaven forbid—married."

"Unfortunately not everyone shares your conviction. What do you have against marriage?"

"Nothing."

They got to his apartment and he dug in his pocket for his keys. "That's not what it sounded like."

"I know, but I only meant that getting married is the ultimate commitment. Not something I would take lightly." She shrugged, glanced briefly at him. "Nor is it on my 'to do' list. Not soon, anyway."

"I understand." That pretty much summed up his feelings, too. He opened the door. "Jeez, I hope it's clean. I haven't paid much attention lately," he said with a perfectly straight face. "I have a woman who comes in once a week—unfortunately that isn't until tomorrow." That part was true.

Dallas walked in and looked around. "You don't need her. This place is cleaner than mine." She gave him a smile that suggested she knew he'd spent an hour picking up his crap and scrubbing the bathroom just before meeting her.

"I'm not here much. I work pretty long hours. Make yourself at home."

"This is really nice." She trailed her hand along the back of the tan Italian-leather couch he'd spent way too much money for. "Did you decorate it yourself?"

"No, not exactly. But I did pick out the furniture." Ashley, a woman Judy had tried to fix him up with, had done most of the decorating. Not at his request. She'd insisted. He'd seen her occasionally for about three months. Great sex. Lousy conversation. Their split was mutual.

"I really like this." Dallas crouched to study the oval glass coffee table with a black iron base that was supported by four wrought-iron legs in the shape of elephant tusks. "Very unusual."

"Yeah, it grabbed me. Hey, about dinner—I'm sorry about the delay. But I have some mixed nuts, if you're interested." He stepped into the small kitchen where he kept several bottles of wine, a bottle of scotch, a can of nuts, a jar of peanut butter and little else.

A brown-and-cream-colored granite-top counter separated the living room from the kitchen. Since there was no dining room area, he'd meant to get a couple of bar stools so the counter could be used as a table—as it had probably been intended—but he hadn't gotten around to it. He never entertained and rarely ate at home, except for maybe cheese and crackers while he sat in front of the television and watched a ball game.

"And wine. You like white, right?" He got out a bottle of chardonnay from the refrigerator. When he turned around, he found that she'd moved to the counter and, with her forearms resting on the granite, leaned toward him.

His mouth went dry and he exhaled slowly. Her neckline gaped enough to give him an excellent view of the tops of her breasts. He knew she wore a bra, but it had to be really low cut, because another inch and he'd be able to see the rosy crowns.

He realized he'd stared too long and he forced his gaze up to her face. She smiled. He cleared his throat and concentrated on opening the can of nuts.

"How did you and Jimmy Chun get to be such good friends?" she asked.

"We aren't really. I've been getting takeout there for about two years. That's all."

Her eyebrows went up. "He apparently has a different perspective."

"I did him a small favor and now he thinks—" Eric rubbed his jaw "—I don't know what he thinks."

"He thinks you're The Man."

"Knock it off or no wine for you."

She laughed. "There's definitely some hero-worship going on there. What did he mean about having so many customers because of you?"

"Nothing," he mumbled and got down the wineglasses.

"Come on. Tell me."

"Are you always this nosy?"

She paused for a moment, as if giving the matter serious thought, her lips pursed in a sexy pout. "No, but I am determined." She shifted, giving him a better look down her blouse. "And you will tell me."

He took a deep breath and looked away. "Uh, what were we talking about?"

She laughed and straightened, taking the bottle he'd abandoned and pouring her own wine. "You were about to tell me what you did for Jimmy."

"Determined, you said. As in stubborn?"

"You got it." She gave him a smile that could seduce every last secret out of him. "Are you having white, too?"

"Sure."

She poured another glass of wine and handed it to him. Her fingers casually brushed his, and damn if his gut didn't tighten. "I'm listening."

He sighed and came around the counter to join her. After they'd both settled on the couch he said, "The place never seemed crowded. Even at peak lunch or dinner hour. And I knew firsthand the food was terrific. Then one day I overheard him talking to his daughter— the one who was at the register. He told her he was thinking of closing, that business just wasn't good enough to stay open. She got all upset, and—" he shrugged, uncomfortable talking about this "—I guess I stuck my nose in it."

Her head tilted slightly to the side, and listening intently, she sat facing him with one leg curled under her bottom. "And?"

He took a sip of his wine. "I'm in advertising. I drew up a simple and low-cost game plan to let people know about the place, designed some flyers and a reward system for referrals. The usual. It was nothing."

Her smile lit up her eyes. "You're a very nice man, you know that?"

"I'm telling you it was no big deal. To tell you the

truth, if I'd known he was going to act like this, I wouldn't have done it." He focused on his watch. "I can't forget to call him."

Uncomfortable with the conversation, he didn't look up for a long time. She was making too big a thing out of this. What he'd done for Jimmy was remedial stuff he'd learned in college. It had been fun. Not like the work he did now, where the enormous pressure to please the client with his first pitch took all the pleasure out of his job.

"All right, we can change the subject," she said, running the toe of her shoe up his calf and taking a sip of her wine, her gaze fastened on him over the rim.

He smiled, set his glass on the coffee table, and then took hers out of her hand. "Come here."

Her lips curved, and she lifted her chin in challenge. "What do you want with me?"

"I'll show you." He wove a hand through her hair, cupping her scalp, and drew her toward him.

Just as their lips met, the phone rang. Eric ignored it but Dallas leaned back.

"Forget it," he whispered. "I'm not expecting a call." He tried to bring her back to him but she resisted.

"Could it be Jimmy? Does he have your number?"

"If it is, he can leave a message."

"Eric…"

He sighed. The mood had obviously disintegrated so he got to his feet. Before he reached the phone, he heard Jimmy's voice leaving a message on the answering machine. Eric muttered a word he shouldn't have and then picked up the phone.

Dallas watched him pace as he spoke to Jimmy. Even though he was obviously frustrated, his tone never revealed his annoyance. After a brief conversation he hung up and returned to the couch.

He shook his head. "He's delivering dinner."

She laughed. "You have a fan. Get over it."

"Remind me never to do any more good deeds." Sighing, he checked his watch. "He'll be here in ten minutes." He trailed a knuckle along her jaw and then tipped her chin up, brushed his lips across hers. "Any suggestions on how we should use the time?"

"You have Scrabble?"

"Funny."

"I—"

He didn't let her finish but pressed his advantage, slipping his tongue through her parted lips. She sort of fell against him, as if he'd just sucked all the energy out of her. Even if she wanted to refuse him, she couldn't muster the strength to pull away.

Not that she had any intention of retreating. The same musky masculine scent that had taunted her last night filled her every pore. His hand swept down her back, lingered at her waist, cupped the swell of her butt. His touch drugged her. Made her feel helpless. Made her want more.

"Take off your blouse," he whispered as he worked his hand beneath the fabric, his warm palm pressed against her skin, his strong fingers trailing up the muscle on either side of her spine.

"Shouldn't we wait for Jimmy?"

He smiled against her mouth. "You're into three-somes?"

Laughing, she leaned back to glare at him. "You know what I mean."

Eric chuckled and then fell back against the couch and groaned. "Damn that Jimmy."

She placed a hand on his thigh and squeezed a little. "Poor baby."

One of his eyebrows went up. "An inch higher and I'll let Jimmy wait in the lobby all night."

"And what about dinner?"

He looked horrified. "You mean we have to eat first?"

Dallas laughed. "First? Did you have something else in mind?"

His mouth curved in a predatory smile. He caught her arm before she could pull away. "I have lots of things in mind. Want to hear about them?"

She shivered and moistened her suddenly parched lips.

He drew her toward him, leaning forward at the same time. "Or would you rather I show you?"

A buzzing sound startled them.

Eric glanced apologetically at her. "Was that ten minutes? That was not ten minutes," he muttered as he got up and went to the door.

On the right was a small silver panel. He depressed a black button and the doorman's voice came through telling him he had a delivery. Eric spoke into the speaker and told him to let Jimmy come up.

Dallas checked her blouse, smoothed back her hair with a shaky hand and in general made sure there were no telltale signs of their fooling around. She didn't expect Eric would allow Jimmy to stay long. Which would be a very good thing. Her insides hadn't quit tingling. If Eric wanted to skip dinner and resume where they'd left off, that was more than okay with her.

He hovered near the door, with it slightly ajar, waiting for Jimmy. She thought she heard the elevator ding, and then Eric reached into his pocket and brought out some money, reminding her this was supposed to be her turn to buy dinner.

"Hey, I'm getting that," she said and pushed off the couch, looking around for where she'd dropped her purse.

"Please, one argument at a time."

"What?" She had no idea what he was talking about, and then Jimmy showed up at the door, carrying a bag of food big enough to feed five people.

She understood as soon as Eric tried to give him the money.

"No, my friend, this is a gift." Jimmy grinned and tried to shove the bag into Eric's arms.

"No way." Eric stepped back, his arms rigidly at his side. "Either I pay for this or you take it back."

Jimmy shook his head, a hurt yet stubborn expression on his face.

Eric stuffed some bills in the man's breast pocket. "Take it, okay, Jimmy? Please." Then Eric took the bag from him, cradled it in his left arm and extended his right hand to Jimmy. "I'll see you in a few days."

Jimmy smiled and stepped back. "Okay," he said and left.

Tom had told her Eric was a rising star with Webber and Thornton Advertising. At the time she'd thought it might be an exaggeration to peak her interest, a ploy to get her to the company party. But she'd heard enough from the other guests Saturday night to make her a believer.

She leaned a hip against the counter beside him. "Mmm, smells divine."

He took a couple of white cartons out of the bag and read the black writing on the side. He set them aside and brought out three more cartons.

"Good grief. That's a lot of food. Enough for a party." She stared at the spread.

"Is that so?"

"Come on now. I offered to share my raw fish with you last night."

He winced. "Thank you very much for the reminder."

Grinning, she opened the carton of pot stickers. The tantalizing aroma made her stomach rumble. "These smell way too good. Is there dipping sauce?"

"I'm sure there is. Not that it matters."

At the odd tone in his voice, she looked over at him. "Excuse me?"

He took the carton out of her hand and set it aside. With a sweep of one arm he cleared the counter, sending the cartons of food up against the microwave. "I believe we have some unfinished business," he said, grasping her by the waist and lifting her onto the counter.

8

SHE COULD BARELY CATCH HER breath. Her heart threatened to explode. He'd taken her by surprise. "Hey, you, I'm wearing white. If I get anything on these pants—"

He smiled and kissed the side of her mouth. "You could always take them off."

She let her head fall back and he kissed her throat, continued on to her collarbone, licking the skin just above her neckline. He spread her legs and stepped closer until he was cradled between her thighs. He cupped her bottom and pulled her against him.

She sighed when he put his mouth on her breast, teasing the nipple with his teeth through the fabric. Automatically she tried to squeeze her thighs together, but he was right there, inches away from her core, where the dampness had started.

Clutching two fistfuls of his shirt, she yanked the hem out of his jeans and pushed it up as far as the shirt would go until he gave in and stepped back so she could finish the job. She tossed the T-shirt toward the couch and it landed on the arm.

He grinned. "Nice throw."

"Nice chest." She slid her palms from his shoulders

over his nipples and down his belly, feeling it clench as she rested at his waistband. "You're a runner, aren't you?"

"I used to log five miles a day. Lately I only get out about three times a week."

She ran her palms back up, and as she grazed his nipples, he briefly closed his eyes. He didn't have a bulky, heavily muscled weight lifter's body. Simply lean and well defined with a light mat of hair—just the way she liked a man's body to look and feel.

"I know. Getting soft. I probably need to join a gym." He picked up a few strands of her hair and rubbed it between his forefinger and thumb. "It's like silk. I've never felt hair this soft and fine before."

He stared at it as if totally mesmerized, letting the strands sift through his fingers and then starting over. His gaze finally switched to her face and he smiled. He let go of her hair and used the back of his hand to touch her face.

"You're definitely not getting soft," she whispered, making another run up his chest, enjoying the feel of soft, springy hair beneath her palms.

His smile got crooked. "A truer statement was never made."

She realized the double entendre in what she'd said and laughed. "Oh, really? I haven't explored that far yet."

"What's keeping you?" He lowered his hands to grab a hold of her blouse and gently drew it over her head. Without looking, he tossed it in the same direction as his shirt. His gaze stayed fastened to her peach satin demicup bra. Or more accurately what spilled out of it.

Under the heat of his gaze, she shivered. The intensity in his eyes penetrated every bone in her body until she didn't think she could keep herself from sliding to the floor. "Why aren't we in the bedroom?"

He trailed a finger over the top of her bra, occasionally slipping inside the cup and grazing her nipple with his fingertip, creating a nearly unbearable friction. "We'll get there. Eventually."

The teasing in his smile told her he knew exactly what he was doing to her. It called her to action, and she slid her palms to his waist and attacked his belt buckle.

He murmured something indistinct. Sucked in his belly and closed his eyes. She freed the buckle and went for his zipper, but he moved out of reach.

Startled, she returned her gaze to his face.

To her satisfaction, he seemed a little shaken himself.

"Oh, man." He exhaled loudly.

"What?"

"Wait. I'll be right back."

She twisted around to see where he was going. He went into the living room and picked up their wineglasses from the coffee table. She swallowed and looked down at herself, suddenly feeling too exposed.

"Bring my blouse, please," she called after him, but it was too late. He'd already entered the kitchen.

Alarm darkened his face. "What's wrong?"

"I thought you—" She shrugged, unwilling to voice her insecurities. "I don't know."

"Here." He handed her the half-empty glass of wine she'd abandoned. "I was abrupt. I'm sorry. No reflection on you, believe me." He got the bottle of chardonnay out of the fridge and then turned back to her with a frown—and one hell of a hard-on. The bulge strained against his fly, and she could barely keep from staring. "I take that back. It's you. You're making me crazy. I need a time-out."

She tried not to smile. "Sorry to hear that."

"Right." Snorting, he poured more wine in each of their glasses. He took a quick sip and then put his glass down beside her on the counter, his hungry gaze drawing to her breasts.

She got that warm, tingly feeling again and prepared herself for his touch. It didn't come. He reached around her and got the carton of pot stickers and a pair of chopsticks.

Last night proved he was quite adept with the wooden utensils, but tonight he fumbled with them, and finally with a sigh of disgust, he cast them aside, fished out one of the dumplings with his fingers and put it to her lips.

She took a small bite, even though she was no longer interested in dinner, and he finished the rest of it.

That she was sitting here wearing only a bra and capris and he was shirtless with his belt unbuckled eating dinner struck her as incredibly funny and she burst out laughing.

He licked the corner of her mouth. "Come on, admit it. This is the way to eat."

"Trying to steal my pot sticker?"

"I'm after more than that."

She was about to utter a smart retort when her stomach grumbled loudly.

He grinned and picked out another dumpling. "All you had to do was ask."

"I'm not really hungry," she murmured, embarrassed. "I don't know why it did that."

"Hungry or not, you need sustenance." He fed her another bite. "We have a long night ahead of us."

She swallowed and moistened her lips, the tingling starting again. "Yeah?"

"Oh, yeah." He locked gazes with her and, after a moment, shoved the carton aside. "The hell with this," he said and scooped her up.

Dallas yelped. At five-nine, she wasn't the type of woman a man easily managed to carry. She tried to maneuver herself down, but he held tight and carried her into the bedroom. There he let her down gently, holding on to her until her feet touched the plush white carpet.

He lifted her chin, kissed her briefly and then unclasped the front of her bra. He stopped for a moment to admire his discovery with a fascination that stole her breath, then he tugged the straps off her shoulders. The bra slid down her back and onto the floor.

Lowering his head, he kissed one rosy tip and then the other. She blossomed against his mouth, ached for him to suckle her, but he took his time, finally leaning back to look at her again.

"Do you have any idea how incredibly beautiful you are?" He seemed a little dazed, astonishingly earnest, and she didn't experience the embarrassment she should have. Didn't make the wisecrack she normally would have about the dim lighting. "Tell me this isn't a dream. You are real, aren't you?"

She lifted herself on tiptoes and kissed him before reaching for his zipper. This time he didn't move. He watched her as she slid the zipper down, exposing brown silk boxers, and then shuddered when she touched him.

"Does this feel real?" she whispered, running the back of her fingers over the hard thickness straining against the silky fabric.

He murmured something, his voice too hoarse to understand. Grabbing her wrists, he forced her hands away. Took a couple of deep breaths, his chest heaving.

"Help me," he said, but she didn't understand until he moved back and yanked one side of the rust-colored quilt back from his queen-size bed.

She took the other side but gave up on trying to be neat about it when he shoved everything to the foot of the bed, heedless of the rich textured fabric that spilled to the floor.

When he reached for the lamp, she started to protest, preferring the filtered light coming from the living room. But he switched it on dim, and the soft glow bathed the coppery tones of the room in a mellow warmth that helped calm her.

"Need help taking those off?" he asked, lowering his gaze to her capris.

She smiled at the nudge. He was already pulling off his jeans. "I think I can manage."

He stepped out of them and then without hesitation he slid off his boxers. She froze and stared. She tried not to. Tried to finish undressing. But she couldn't seem to move. He was truly beautiful. Breathtaking, really.

Swallowing hard, trying to get in motion, she told herself that he wasn't the best-looking guy she'd dated. In fact, she'd dated some real honeys. One of them a famous local model who'd had a terrific sense of humor. But something about Eric appealed to her like none of the others. Something beyond his good looks and generosity and sense of humor. Maybe it was simple chemistry. Maybe it was about this crazy mystery-woman fantasy of hers.

"I guess you do need some help," he said, discarding the boxers and approaching her.

She still couldn't move. Until he was right there. In front of her. And she reached out and touched him. His penis twitched at the contact, and when she circled the glistening tip, he shuddered. She curled her hand around it and stroked down to the base, and he moaned.

A sense of power surged through her, and finding a rhythm, she started to pump him, but he captured her wrist and stilled her hand.

"Wait, Dallas," he said, his breathing irregular.

She smiled. "Whatever for?"

"This." He lowered his head and took control of her mouth, forcing her lips open with his tongue.

She didn't move when he released her wrist and slid his hands around to her backside, squeezing gently while he kissed her senseless. It took a few moments before she realized he was sliding her capris down her hips, past her thighs.

He broke the kiss to pull them down her legs and stopped to nuzzle her breasts, swirling his tongue around one nipple and then the other. She shuddered and grabbed his shoulder, and he held her steady while she stepped out of the capris.

Standing in only a skimpy pair of cream-colored silk bikini panties, she sucked in a breath when he moved back to look at her. Appreciation gleamed in his eyes as his gaze swept her body, lingering at the small, silky triangle at the juncture of her thighs.

"Take those off," he whispered hoarsely, lowering his hands to his sides, his fists clenching lightly.

She obeyed by slipping her hands beneath the strips of lacy elastic across her hips and then slowly lowering her panties, her palms molding her skin as she slid the silky fabric down her thighs, taking her time, making him wait.

Visibly swallowing, he watched her, his chest rising and falling, his gaze riveted to her little striptease show. His hand went to his straining sex and he touched himself briefly before backing her up so that she fell on the bed. He sprawled over her, hungrily kissing her mouth, her cheek, her eyelids, as if it were impossible for him not to.

She moved her hips and his breathing faltered. He wrapped his arms around her and rolled onto his back, bringing her with him. Her hair fell forward, brushing his chest, and he pushed one side back from her face and rubbed the pad of his thumb across her cheek.

"So soft," he whispered. "So incredibly soft."

She reached between them, stroking his penis. "So hard. So incredibly hard."

He laughed, an abrupt gurgling sound, before rolling her back into position beneath him. "Okay, you asked for it."

She smiled. "Yes, I did."

To her surprise, he turned away. But then she saw that he'd reached into the nightstand and brought out a foil packet. He ripped it open and then handed it to her. She didn't know why it never came up, but she'd never actually done this before. The guy she was with always had.

Carefully she rolled the condom down the hard thickness, smiling when he reacted with a small jerk, his stomach clenching.

"Amused, are we?" he asked, his smile turning feral before he held her hands out wide and touched the tip of his tongue to her nipples ever so lightly. Just enough to make her crazy.

Then before she knew what had happened, he'd spread her thighs. Increasing the pressure of his mouth on her nipples, he explored her with his hand, gently probed her with his fingers until she clenched around them.

She wanted him inside her so badly, she must have somehow communicated it to him. With a guttural groan he positioned himself over her and slid inside with precise aim, as if this were their hundredth time. She bucked at the initial contact, tensing, until she adjusted to the size and feel of him.

He slowly withdrew, never breaking contact, and

then thrust deeper. She shuddered and wrapped her legs around his waist, pulling him impossibly closer. Her response ignited him and he thrust faster, deeper, the muscles in his arms and shoulders straining as he held himself poised above her.

She clenched tightly around him and he groaned, started to withdraw, but she wouldn't have it and lifted her hips to stay joined with him. Clearly realizing her intention, he whispered her name and then thrust into her again and again and again until the first wave hit her. She turned her head into the pillow to keep from making too much noise as the convulsions nearly sent her flying off the bed.

He had no such restraint. He cried out as he climaxed, pounding against her, meeting her thrust for thrust until he collapsed on top of her, panting her name and showering her face with kisses.

Dallas lay back, boneless and spent, unable to catch her breath. Eric kissed her a final time on the mouth and then fell onto his back, sounding just as breathless.

"Wow," he said.

"Yeah, wow." She smiled and laid a hand on his thigh. "Double wow."

Chuckling, he rolled over to face her. "What are you doing tomorrow night? I know a great Italian restaurant."

She smiled at his amazing ability to recover. "I can't. I've got something going on tomorrow evening."

"How about Wednesday? Are we still on for my client's reception?"

"Sure."

He lay back with one arm behind his head, looked at her and gave her a smile that made her insides tingle. "Is seven okay with you?"

"Whatever time you think we should be there."

"I'll pick you up at your place around six forty-five."

She shook her head. "I'll meet you there at seven."

He didn't like it, given the sudden frown that drew his brows together.

She snuggled against him and toyed with the hair on his chest. "What's the address?"

"Trying to distract me?" He turned onto his side and curled an arm around her, hauling her against his chest. "You have to do better than that."

She reached between them and found him growing hard again. "Am I getting warmer?"

His laugh was shaky. "I am."

"It's almost midnight. I really should be going," she said, curling her hand around him and feeling him twitch.

"I don't think so."

Before she could reply, he had her on her back, her wrists pinned to the pillows, and she knew she wasn't going anywhere anytime soon.

DALLAS SLOWLY OPENED HER EYES. She blinked at the unfamiliar teak armoire and the valet beside it. The walls were painted a taupe color. Not white. This wasn't her room. Where the hell was she?

She felt movement in the bed. Warm skin brushed her bare back. Remembering where she was and who was curled against her, she smiled. Briefly she closed her eyes again. How could she have fallen asleep? She really had to go home. She still had some work to do for the meeting tomorrow evening. *Just another few minutes,* she decided and slowly turned over to face him.

Eric was still asleep, his lips slightly parted, his chin dark with stubble. She instantly recalled the slightly rough feel on her bare breasts and shivered.

He stirred and she lay quiet, waiting with mixed emotions to see if he'd waken. If he did, they'd probably go a third round. As enticing as that sounded, they both had to get up early tomorrow and he had a big presentation to make to a new client.

Her gaze went to the digital alarm clock and she bit back a curse. It was already after one-thirty. She had to go. No more fooling around. She slowly slipped out of bed and quietly gathered her clothes in the dark. To avoid waking him, she carried everything to the bathroom and dressed there.

When she was finished, she went to the kitchen, where she'd seen a notepad by the phone. She thought for a moment about what she wanted to say and then scribbled him a note.

The obvious place to have left it would be on her vacated pillow, but she dared not wake him. Instead she anchored a corner of the paper under the coffeemaker and then she grabbed her purse. She got to the door, hesitated and then, cursing herself under her breath, snuck back to his room for a final irresistible peek.

He was still sound asleep, his beautiful chest bare,

the sheet bunched at his waist. Tempted to crawl back in beside him, she took a deep breath and then backed away from the door. With foolish reluctance, she let herself out.

9

DALLAS FILLED TWO PITCHERS with water and set them next to the coffeepot on the credenza against the wall. She counted the number of chairs at the long conference table and hoped twelve would be enough. Then again, if they weren't, that would still be a good thing. The first meeting had been held at her apartment, but the number of women interested in improving their work conditions had swelled to the point that Dallas could no longer accommodate everyone.

Fortunately her sister had offered the conference room at the law firm where she worked. Like the rest of the family, Dakota thought Dallas was nuts for shunning her MBA and choosing manual labor. But at least she accepted Dallas's choice and was sympathetic to the plight of women who worked in male-dominated jobs. She was also the least snobby of the Shea clan. Although she had her moments.

Dallas checked her watch. The women would start arriving at any minute. She unwrapped the tray of cookies she'd picked up at the corner bakery.

"Hey." Dakota poked her head in. "Everything okay?"

"Perfect." Dallas waved her inside. "Change your mind about staying for the meeting?"

"I can't." She glanced at her watch. "I have a class in forty minutes."

"You're teaching again?"

"Just a couple of summer courses."

"Like you don't have your hands full enough here."

"No lectures." Dakota glared, but she couldn't manage to keep the corners of her mouth from curving slightly. "*I* get paid to give them. That makes me a professional. Don't mess with me."

Dallas grinned at her younger sister. "Glad to see some of the old fire in you again."

"Don't go there."

"What?"

"I like what I'm doing, okay?"

"I'm sure you do."

"God, you know how much I hate that passive-aggressive tone—" Dakota stopped and stared at Dallas in disbelief. "You sounded just like Mom."

"Funny," she said and muttered a curse.

"Seriously. You totally sounded like her."

Dallas bristled and turned away to pour herself a cup of coffee. Of all the insults Dakota could have hurled, that was the lowest.

"No, really. I'm not trying to be obnoxious." She shrugged. "You really sounded like her."

Dallas sighed.

"But only for a second."

They looked at each other and laughed. It felt good.

Just like the old days. Before Dakota had gotten so caught up in her career that she forgot to enjoy life. Just like the rest of the family.

"You want a cup of coffee?" Dallas asked.

"Nope. You know I don't drink that nasty stuff. Anyway, I gotta go." Dakota checked her watch again and then abruptly brought her head up. "I almost forgot. Mom wants us all to come to the house for dinner on Saturday."

Great. "What's the occasion?"

Dakota shrugged. "I think she just wants to see everyone."

"I think I can make it. I'll check my calendar."

Dakota hesitated, her serious gray eyes tentative. She obviously wanted to say something. Probably in defense of their mother's dominating edicts. The woman never made requests. They were more like demands. And Andrea Shea expected unconditional compliance.

To her credit, she'd taught her daughters self-sufficiency, the importance of an education and to never trade on their looks. Dakota could have easily made it in modeling. With her honey-colored hair, gray eyes and wide smile, she was perfect for the camera. A real natural. But she'd been a serious and bright student who'd never given her appearance a second thought, much less attempted to parlay her looks into a career.

"Dallas, I'd really like it if you came. We haven't had a family dinner in a while."

A soft knock at the door drew their attention. It was one of the women with whom Dallas worked. Dressed in clean jeans and a white cotton shirt, Nancy smiled shyly. "I guess this is the place."

"Yep. Come in." Dallas motioned her inside. "You're the first one. I'm really glad you came."

"I'll see you later," Dakota said, acknowledged Nancy with a quick smile and then disappeared before Dallas could introduce them.

"How about some coffee?" Dallas set her cup down and picked up a clean mug.

"Sure." Nancy glanced around the conference room, admiring the dark polished wood, the pair of Georgia O'Keeffe paintings on the cream-colored walls. Beyond the expansive windows was a spectacular twilight view of midtown. She walked closer to the glass. "Wow!"

"Do you take cream and sugar?"

"Just sugar," Nancy said absently and then blinked at her. "Oh, I'll get that. You don't have to wait on me."

"I get you the first cup, then you're on your own." Dallas added the sugar and then handed her the mug.

She accepted it, her eyes inquiring as they locked with Dallas's. "Tony said you went to college."

"Yes," she said slowly, not wanting to invite conversation on the subject but not wanting to seem rude either. "So did he."

"Yeah, but he dropped out after two years. He says you even have a graduate degree."

"There are cookies here, too. The chocolate-chunk ones are awesome." She was gonna smack that big-mouth Tony.

Nancy shook her head. Her brown hair, still a little

damp, hung down around her shoulders instead of being pulled up in her usual work ponytail. "I don't get it. If I didn't have to do such a dirty job, I sure as heck wouldn't be out there sweating every day. I'd even rather waitress if it weren't for Petey." She shrugged. "When you got a kid and no husband, you gotta make sure the money is steady coming in."

"I understand. But that doesn't mean you have to put up with the kind of abuse those jerks dish out. That's why we're here tonight."

Nancy's face darkened and she hunched her shoulders. "No one knows about the meeting, do they? I can't afford to get fired."

"Number one, they can't fire you for this. That would be illegal. Number two, none of the guys know unless one of the women told them."

"Who opened their friggin' big mouth?" Jan walked in, shrugging off her backpack. She still wore her work jeans and boots. Her short dark hair hadn't been washed but merely slicked back. "I'll take care of 'em."

"No one." Dallas sighed. That's all they needed. Jan was a loose cannon with enough muscle and attitude to cause some damage. Rumor had it that she'd decked one of the forklift drivers and sent him to the hospital. "I was just reassuring Nancy. That's all."

Three other women who Dallas vaguely recognized walked in together. They all worked for Capshaw's Construction, too, but they were part of a crew that worked on the Upper East Side, which meant word was spreading.

Dallas ushered them toward the coffee and cookies

and then poked her head out the door to glance down the hall. Another woman had just stepped out of the elevator. Alone. Not good. Apparently word wasn't spreading quickly enough. It was already ten minutes past the time the meeting was supposed to start.

"Hey, are we gonna start soon? I only got a babysitter for three hours," a short, stocky blonde said between bites of cookie. "And I already used up one of them."

"Let's wait five more minutes, okay?" Dallas foolishly checked her watch again. Only seconds had passed. Where the hell was everybody? From the responses she'd received, she'd been so sure of a larger turnout. But that was the basic problem. Their initial enthusiasm always seemed to evaporate into fear.

After ten more minutes of eating and chatting and exploring the conference room, the women began to get restless, and Dallas decided it was best to get started.

They all took seats and went around the table introducing themselves. Even though they all worked for Capshaw's Construction, they worked for different crews and knew each other casually.

"Okay," Dallas said after the room got quiet. "Who wants to volunteer to lead the meeting?"

Six blank faces stared back at her and then they glanced nervously at each other.

Jan spoke first. "I thought this was your party."

Dallas shook her head. "This gender problem doesn't belong to any particular individual. That's the reason for this meeting—to pull together to decide what action we should take. There's strength in numbers."

"We already have a union." Jan snorted. "Not that they give a rat's ass about us."

"Look," Dallas said, "we need to make a stand together. Neither the union nor Capshaw's Construction can ignore us if we make a joint statement."

"But they can fire us." Nancy clasped her hands so tightly that her nails dug into her skin.

"No, they can't." Dallas gave her a reassuring smile. "That would leave them wide open for a lawsuit."

"They'll still give us a bad time," Sally said, her freckled face flushed. She looked twelve and sweet. Amazing what came out of her mouth. "I get enough shit from those pigs as it is."

"Individually, yes, I agree, it's hard to stop the harassment. It's your word against theirs. But what I'm suggesting is that we all sign an informal complaint and give the powers that be an opportunity to talk to the men. Legally, once they know the harassment exists, they have to address the problem and make sure it stops."

"You mean like put our names in writing?" Nancy asked, clearly horrified at the thought.

Dallas hesitated. She didn't want them all running out of the room. "That's something we have to discuss further."

"I have a question," Yvette said. A quiet woman with sad brown eyes and a heart-shaped face who hadn't said anything since introducing herself, she seemed the most reluctant attendee.

"Yes?" Dallas prompted.

"What if the person giving you trouble is your supervisor?"

"That don't mean nothing. He can't do that." Jan's fists clenched. "Right, Shea?"

"Of course not. It makes the harassment even more despicable. He could be fired for that. Have you discussed the problem with anyone higher up?"

Yvette's eyes widened. "Goodness no. He would have fired *me!*"

"Bullshit! Tell her, Shea." Jan's face reddened with anger. "Tell me who he is. I'll kick his ass."

"Jan," Dallas said softly. "We have the law on our side. There's no need for violence or threats. We just need to stick together to become more effective."

"That's why I'm here," Jan said. "None of them guys bother me." A couple of the women chuckled, and even Jan grinned. "But I see how those pigs act with some of you, and it sucks. It ain't right. I wanna back you up."

"Thank you, Jan." Dallas nodded at her. "We appreciate your courage and support."

"I got a question for you, Shea." Jan studied Dallas for a moment with a hint of suspicion in her eyes and then asked, "Why are you here? Somebody told me you used to model and you went to college. You don't need to do this stinkin' job."

All gazes riveted to Dallas. They all had the same question in their eyes, the same suspicion. Total honesty was required. And owed them.

Dallas cleared her throat. "Yes, I once modeled and

I do have a college degree, and in fact, I have a graduate degree in business. But I hated the pressure of modeling and I realized the path I'd taken in school had been
to please my parents. To be perfectly honest, I don't
know what I want to do." She smiled wryly. "Except that
I don't want to work in construction all my life."

They all snorted and glanced at each other.

"I admit this is temporary for me, a way to earn a living until I figure out what I want to do." That her parents considered her choice an act of defiance was merely
a bonus. But she didn't want to share that tidbit. "But I
still want to help improve the work conditions for
women who choose this job."

"Or have no choice," Yvette said miserably.

"It's not a bad job," Jan said, shrugging. "You go
home at the end of the day and that's it. No worries."

"Yeah, right," Nancy said irritably.

"I didn't mean nothin'. I get it that the guys give you
a hard time." Jan sighed loudly. "I'm just sayin'…"

Dallas slumped in her seat. "How about we try to be
a little more constructive?"

The meeting continued for another hour but with little progress. They all agreed on only two things. One
was to think about what had been discussed and then
meet again the following week. The second was that
Dallas should lead the charge. Too bad she had no idea
what to do next.

DALLAS LET HERSELF INTO HER apartment and sighed
with relief when she realized Wendy wasn't home.

They got along great. Rarely disagreed. But tonight had been horrendously draining, and all Dallas wanted to do was stretch out with a glass of wine. And talk to Eric.

No. Bad idea. She'd be likely to spill too much of her frustration with work. Share her disappointment. Let him get too close. That would be totally foolish. Disastrous. A great way to ruin the fantasy.

She kicked off her shoes and poured herself half a glass of wine, when she'd really like to down half the bottle. She stared at the jagged nail on her index finger and gritted her teeth. None of her fingernails were long but she kept them at a decent enough length for an occasional French manicure. Today she'd spent four hours sanding walls. Ever so carefully, with gloves on. Then five minutes before she'd knocked off, there went the nail.

Normally she wouldn't care, but tomorrow evening was the reception with Eric. She looked at the phone. Maybe she should call to confirm. If plans had changed, he couldn't call her. She still hadn't given him her number.

She took a sip of wine, telling herself that was an excuse. She could wait until tomorrow to talk to him. Anyway, he was probably working. Drumming her fingers on the counter, she glanced from the phone to the clock and then back to the phone. Two minutes. That's it. *Just to confirm tomorrow evening,* she told herself and grabbed the receiver.

With her purse slung over her shoulder and carrying the glass of wine in one hand, the phone in the other, she headed for her room. She gave herself a few more minutes to change her mind about calling while she kicked off her shoes and turned down her lemon-yellow comforter.

Her room was too tiny to hold anything more than a twin bed, a nightstand and a small dresser, so she plumped her pillow and positioned it against the wall and then made herself comfortable, sitting cross-legged with her back against the pillow.

After another sip of wine, she took a deep breath and dialed his number. She knew it by heart after a glance. It was an easy one to remember.

She let the phone ring three times and was about to hang up when he answered. His voice sounded hoarse, husky, as if he'd been sleeping, but it was only eight-thirty.

"Hey, Eric."

"Dallas?"

"Yeah, did I wake you?"

"No, of course not. I'm glad you called."

"Yeah?" She smiled, her misgivings dissolving.

"I wish you hadn't disappeared last night."

"I didn't exactly disappear. I just didn't want to wake you. Besides, I left a note."

"You should've woken me."

She smiled at the drop in his voice. "Why?"

"I had something for you."

An image of him standing naked in front of her last night instantly flashed in her mind. "I can't imagine what that could have been."

"Come over now and I'll show you."

Laughing, she put her glass on the nightstand and then slid into a horizontal position. "I bet."

"Where are you?"

"At home."

"What are you wearing?"

"A big, bulky white chenille robe and pink curlers in my hair."

"Ah, my older-woman fantasy come to life."

Dallas smiled and rolled over to her side. "I just got home from my meeting."

"How did it go?"

"Pretty horrible."

"Sorry to hear that. Want to tell me about it?"

She bit her lip, annoyed that she'd allowed the conversation to go in that direction. "No, I want to talk about something more pleasant."

"Okay," he said slowly, "let's get back to what you're really wearing."

"You mean besides the G-string?"

After a long moment of silence he said, "You're kidding, right?"

"It's black. Not that you can see much of it."

After another pause he asked, "What did you say your address was?"

She laughed. "Nice try."

"Yeah," he said, sounding a little put off. "Or you could come here."

"It's late."

"It's only eight-forty."

"I have to get up early."

"So do I."

"We wouldn't get any sleep."

He laughed. "Like I'm going to get any now."

"Good point."

"Tell you what, where are you?"

"At home, really."

"No, I mean right now."

"In my room, lying on my bed."

"Perfect."

She sucked in a breath, suddenly aware of where this was going. "Why?"

"Take off your clothes."

Heat spiraled through her. "And?"

"Take them off and then I'll give you further instructions."

She hesitated, momentarily self-conscious, but excitement at the prospect of what could come moved her to do as he asked, and she unbuttoned her jeans.

"Dallas?"

"Yes?"

"Tell me what you're doing."

"Taking my clothes off as you asked."

"Be specific."

She laughed, a little self-conscious again.

"Tell me," he urged, his voice growing hoarse.

"My jeans," she whispered, her hands starting to tremble. "I'm pulling down the zipper."

"Go on."

"I'm pushing the jeans down past my hips." She cradled the phone between her chin and shoulder as she struggled to free herself of the stubborn denim.

"Are they off yet?"

"Almost." The phone slipped as she shoved the jeans to her ankles. She kicked them off and repositioned the receiver. "Okay."

"Are you wearing panties?"

"Of course." She laughed. It came out shaky.

"Describe them."

"They're black."

"Silk?"

"Yes," she lied. Plain cotton wasn't sexy and she was really getting into the game.

"A thong?"

"Yes."

He moaned, the sound low and raspy and shooting straight down her spine. "Take them off."

"They're already off."

He breathed deeply into the phone. "Now your blouse."

"I'll have to put the phone down."

"Leave it where I can hear you."

She sat up and took a quick sip of wine. "You, too. Take off your clothes."

His laugh was more a low, sexy growl. "Baby, I'm way ahead of you."

"You're naked?"

"Almost. Down to boxers."

She smiled as she unbuttoned her blouse. "What color?"

"Don't ruin the mood."

"Come on. Play fair."

He hesitated. "Black with red chili peppers."

She laughed. "Really?"

"They were a gag gift from a friend."

"Wear them often?"

"Only when I haven't done laundry for two weeks." He sighed. "Can we get back to something more interesting?"

"Such as?"

"Your bra. Take it off."

"You've assumed I'm wearing one."

Silence, and then he said, "You're not?"

She smiled, picturing the way his eyes darkened and his nostrils flared slightly when he was aroused but trying to hold back. Funny how he seemed so clear in her mind, as if they'd shared more than one night together. "It's black, silk and lace, and I'm about to unclasp it."

"Do it."

"Done." She slipped one strap off her shoulder and then the other, and the bra fell away.

"You're naked?"

"Oh, yeah." She lay back down and stretched out, resting her palm on her tummy. "You?"

"Uh-huh," Eric murmured. "God, I close my eyes and I can see you. Your nipples. They're pink. Not rose or flesh-colored but really pink."

Suddenly so were her cheeks. She was glad he couldn't see them. Curious, she glanced down at herself. Her nipples were rather pink.

"See what I mean?" he asked as if he could see

through the phone. "They're so soft, too. Like satin. Touch them."

Dallas sucked in a breath.

"Come on. Touch them and tell me what you feel."

She moistened her lips. Slowly drew the tips of two fingers around the areola and then pinched the hardened nipple between her thumb and forefinger, closing her eyes, imagining Eric's hand on her body. She bit her lower lip.

"Dallas?" Throaty and hoarse, his voice came across the phone line in a whisper. "Tell me."

She couldn't speak at first. The intimacy of what they were doing amazed her. How could she feel so safe with Eric? The idea was absurd, but there it was. "What I'm feeling has nothing to do with my fingertips."

He started to laugh, too, and then gasped and moaned in her ear. A sensual moan that told her he was also pleasing himself.

The idea excited her further and she slipped her other hand between her thighs. "Tell me what you're doing." She closed her eyes, picturing him in her mind's eye.

"Stroking my cock," he said without hesitation. "Pretending it's you lying here touching me."

She shuddered. If he was trying to tempt her into going over to his place, he was doing a damn good job. "Are you hard yet?"

"Oh, baby." His laugh came out shaky, almost a pant. "Where are your hands?"

"I'm touching my nipples."

"That's not your hands. That's my mouth on you.

Suckling you, licking you." He moaned softly. "I can taste you."

Her eyes still closed, she bit her lip, squeezed her thighs together.

"Your other hand," he whispered, his voice growing more ragged. "Slide your palm down your belly and spread your legs."

She swallowed, took an uneven breath. Did as he ordered. Her fingers grazed the slick wet folds and a moan escaped her.

"That's it. Push a finger inside. Deep."

She tensed around herself and whimpered.

"Now two fingers."

With a trembling hand she inserted another finger.

"Baby, I'm with you. My cock is in your warm mouth." He groaned. "Damn it, I can't hold out much longer."

Dallas heard the front door open. It was Wendy. "I have to go."

"No. Don't." He groaned louder this time. "Touch your clit. Do you feel my tongue?" And louder still. "Ah, Dallas, I can't wait any longer. Baby, come with me."

She closed her eyes, shut out the kitchen noises Wendy was making and imagined Eric bent over her, his face between her legs. The spasms came instantly. She tried to muffle her moans. Heard Eric's anguished release. Heard him whisper her name. She curled onto her side and buried her face into the pillow.

10

ERIC WAITED AT THE DESIGNATED rendezvous point, a feeling of dread knotting the muscles in his neck and shoulders. It wasn't as if he didn't expect her to show up. She'd promised to go to the reception with him and she'd be here. Dallas wasn't the type to stand him up. He didn't know how he knew that exactly. He just did.

Hell, he didn't know her at all. Only what he'd fantasized about her late at night when he tried like hell to get some sleep or while he sat in his office staring out the window when he should have been working on a new ad campaign for Whompie's Burgers.

He'd made it in time in spite of the fact that traffic had been a bitch. A light drizzle had people lined up along both Columbus Avenue and Seventy-second, trying to hail cabs that were all full and passing them by without slowing down. He hoped Dallas wasn't caught up in the mess or that she'd decided it wasn't worth coming out. Nah, he reminded himself, she wouldn't chump him.

He checked his cell phone in case he'd missed a call but there was no message. Then he checked his watch. Not that he gave a damn about the reception. He just wanted to see her. Touch her hair, her soft skin. For real. Last night had been torture. He'd wanted her so badly, he could taste her. Smell her sweet feminine scent. He closed his eyes. He could taste her now.

That and the thought of their phone play last night made him shift from foot to foot, willing his arousal to subside. He didn't dare look down. No sense calling attention to the bulge growing behind his fly. He adjusted his suit jacket to hide his juvenile reaction and then squinted to see who was getting out of a yellow cab stopped at the corner.

Dallas jumped out and darted for cover under the eaves of a diner. He cringed at the black stiletto heels she wore and prayed she didn't break anything in her haste. She made it in one piece, her long, slender legs eating up the wet pavement in four long strides.

Amazing that she could look so graceful dashing through the rain like that, her hair all twisted up with fly-away tendrils that brushed her pink cheeks. In fact, she looked stunning. The whole scene was so perfect, it looked staged. As if it had been set up to shoot a commercial.

It wasn't his imagination. He wasn't the only one staring. Three businessmen who'd just left the diner stood gawking at her. Even a young woman with green spiked hair waiting at the bus stop gave her a second look. The slinky black dress alone was enough to turn heads.

He raised a hand to get her attention. She waved back and then darted across the street between cars. Astonishingly no one honked.

"Hey," she said, smiling, a little breathless—a little

shy, if he wasn't mistaken. Probably because of their phone sex last night. Hell, thinking about it still shook him up. He'd never done anything like that before. But with her it had felt natural, comfortable, incredibly erotic.

God, he couldn't go there right now and risk another hard-on. He took her hand, drew her under cover and briefly kissed her. Difficult as it was to pull away, he reared back and smiled. "Sorry about the rain."

Her eyebrows went up. "You can control the weather? Who knew?"

Pleased that she hadn't shied away, he drew her close again and whispered, "You'd be surprised at what I can do given the right incentive."

She lifted her chin, excitement sparkling in her eyes. "Maybe we ought to skip the reception."

"I have no problem with that." Actually his boss would kill him. This client was too important.

She lightly punched his arm. "I didn't get all dressed up for nothing."

He snorted. "Hey, I think I'm offended."

"I'm sure you'll get over it." She smiled. "Tell me again what this reception is for."

"A client just bought a small strip mall and this is his way of announcing the deal."

She reared her head back. "In Manhattan?"

"No." He had to laugh. "Suburban New Jersey. Some small town. I can't even remember the name of it." At her look of surprise he added, "I'm not working up any ads for the project. Not yet, anyway. The guy likes to party. Any excuse will do."

She nodded thoughtfully. "His name?"

"Lawrence Horn."

She repeated it and nodded again. "Any other names I should know?"

"Uh, no." The serious look on her face fascinated him—as if she were about to enter a boardroom instead of attend a meaningless party. Of course, this wasn't exactly meaningless for him, and that she obviously was preparing herself on his behalf sent a strange tingle down his spine.

The drizzle turned to a sudden downpour, startling them. He shrugged out of his jacket and draped it over her shoulders.

"No, keep it. You'll get soaked."

He stopped her from returning the jacket. "Better me than you."

"This dress will dry in a flash. See?" She pinched the fabric at her neckline between her thumb and finger. "It's that kind of material."

He stared at the creamy skin briefly exposed by her tugging. The dress was clingy enough. Wet, it would be like a second skin. Shouldn't think about that. Couldn't. Not now. "We don't have far to go. Just two doors down. Come on."

She moved her arm away when he tried to take it, her lips curving in a seductive smile. "We could wait a few moments. See if the rain lets up."

"Yeah, okay, sure," he said as she crowded him, forcing him back so that he ended up with his back against the brick retaining wall that hid the alley.

She grabbed a handful of his shirt and pulled his head down so that their lips met. But only briefly, and then she looked up at him and smiled. "Think they'll miss you if we're a little late?"

His cock had already started to respond enthusiastically, and he didn't give a damn if they showed up at all. The client would survive. Eric might not. He took a deep breath. "What did you have in mind?"

"A little of this…" She brushed her lips across his. "A little of that," she whispered breathily near his ear as she moved her hips against his.

Between the heavy rain and small alcove they'd found, someone would have to try hard to see them. If anyone were that nosy, the hell with them. Maybe they'd get an education.

"Oh, my." She brushed her hand down his fly. "What have we here?"

"You're sadistic." He barely got the words out through clenched teeth, afraid he was going to lose it right here in public.

She sighed. "Masochistic, actually."

Buoyed with satisfaction from her admission, he lowered his head and gently bit her lower lip. She whimpered, and he sucked the slick flesh into his mouth. She had something that tasted like strawberries on her lip, but it might as well have been a debilitating drug. His head got light and then heavy, and common sense seemed to evaporate like the wintry morning mist hovering over Long Island Sound under the hot sun.

She moaned and pressed closer. He ran his palms down her back and then cupped her round bottom. She plunged her tongue into his mouth, and his fingers dug into her buttocks as he pulled her hard against his erection.

"Eric." With a shaky laugh she straightened and took a step back. "This is crazy. This is—" Her gaze slid past him. "Look, it stopped raining."

He looked over his shoulder. Mostly it had. Doubtful it would get much better than the persistent light drizzle that continued to mess up traffic.

"Guess we should make a run for it," he said, annoyed that he once again had to cool off a horrendous hard-on.

"I guess so."

"Ready?"

She touched the corner of her mouth. "Do I have lipstick all over my face?"

He licked the spot. "Not anymore."

"Oh, God, don't start."

He breathed deeply. "Yeah, I know."

"We're headed that way, right?" she said, pointing toward Amsterdam Avenue.

"Yep. The red door."

"Here's your jacket."

"Keep it until we get inside."

"Okay, and then I'm going straight to the ladies' room." She smoothed her dress over her hips, and he had to look away. "I'll find you after that."

"I'll be waiting right outside. Ready?"

"Let's go."

He took her arm and steered her around a crack in the sidewalk. Selfishly he liked that she wore the sexy shoes, but he didn't want to see her break any limbs. Even a small nick marring those incredible legs would be a crime.

They got to the door, which was promptly opened by a doorman standing discreetly off to the side. With a sweep of his hand he directed them toward the right, and they followed the strip of red carpet that obviously had been laid for the occasion.

Good thing. Or Eric wouldn't have known which way to go. The brownstone had once been a mansion belonging to one of New York's rich and prominent families, but the building had been gutted and divided into several exclusive shops and a pricey art gallery.

"I haven't seen a restroom, have you?" Dallas whispered.

"Nope, but we'll find it."

"This place is huge. You'd never know it from the outside."

"There it is." He heard classical music coming from the end of the hall and figured that's where they were ultimately headed. "I'll wait right outside."

"I won't be long. Unless damage assessment proves otherwise."

He frowned, not getting it at first, and then he grinned and snatched her hand before she got away. "Come here."

"Why?"

He pulled her close enough that she had to tilt her

head back to look at him. "You still have some lipstick on that I haven't licked off."

She laughed and started to pull away, but he captured her mouth with his and, taking advantage of her soft gasp, slid his tongue between her lips. Without hesitation she looped her arms around his neck and pressed herself against him.

Ridiculous how quickly and how hard he got. A smart man would back off. He pushed his tongue deeper into her mouth, exploring the soft, wet flesh, her perfect teeth. He drew his palms down each side of her body, outlining her seductive curves.

Voices coming from the hall behind them brought him to his senses. He broke the kiss, his breathing already out of control. "Go," he said. "I'll be here."

She nodded, her lower lip quivering slightly, and then she disappeared inside. The voices got closer and he realized he needed a quick adjustment himself so he ducked into the men's room.

What the hell had happened to his focus? What the hell had happened to him? This was absurd. Acting like a kid at a client's function. He knew better. He should never have brought her here.

After finishing his business, he left the restroom to find her already waiting outside. Her frown immediately turned into a smile when she saw him, and all his misgivings vanished just like that.

"I thought maybe you'd decided to go on inside," she said, her lips tinted peach again, some of the stray tendrils of hair tucked back into place.

He liked the wild look better. Reminded him of the way her hair had fanned out against his sheets. There he went again...shit! "Let's go mingle."

She unnecessarily clutched the tiny black bag that hung from her shoulder, as if unsure what to do with her hands. Wisely he kept his to himself. Obviously he couldn't be trusted to touch her. Once they joined the party it would be easier to get through the evening. Especially since he had no intention of staying long.

They entered the large reception area bordering the art gallery and a well-known jewelry store that sold unique baubles that Eric's annual salary couldn't cover. The room was attractive but staid, furnished with over-stuffed chairs and sofas, antique rugs on the floor and rich dark wood paneling on the walls.

In the corner was a humidor with a collection of expensive cigars and floor-to-ceiling racks of wine, probably French and cost prohibitive. At least for Eric. The place looked more like an old gentleman's club from the seventies, when they could still exclude women without ending up in court.

Apparently the rain had either scared some of the guests off or else they were delayed. Less than twenty people stood talking and sipping from martini glasses or champagne flutes. Lawrence's "little" bashes were known to include a hundred or more guests.

"Amazing, isn't it? From the street you'd never know this place existed," Dallas whispered.

"Not really my thing," he whispered back. "But I had to make a showing. I promise we won't stay long."

"I'm not complaining. Really." She looked at him in surprise. "I understand you have to be here. I'm glad you included me."

Eric blinked. It just occurred to him that he'd done exactly what he never did. Never wanted to do. He'd brought a date to a business function. Of course, this was somewhat different from a company party, and Dallas...well, Dallas was certainly different from his other dates.

The thought stopped him. Where had it come from? Why was she different? How? He barely knew her. Yet he felt it deep down in his gut. She was different.

"Eric? What's wrong?"

He stared into her concerned eyes. "Nothing. I was just— Who are you?"

Her face turned guarded. "What do you mean?"

"I know Tom set up Saturday night." He looked closely for her reaction, but she kept her expression neutral. "We saw you in the window."

"What window?"

He smiled. "Come on, Dallas, the joke is over."

"Eric."

At the sound of Lawrence Horn's voice Eric reluctantly broke eye contact with Dallas, and turned to his client—his long-standing, major-revenue-producing client, to whom Eric would do well to be paying attention.

The guy had over a dozen thriving businesses in the New York and New Jersey area and had used Webber and Thornton for two decades, long before Eric had joined the company. It had been an honor for Eric to be entrusted with the account. He wasn't about to blow it.

"Lawrence, good to see you." Eric extended his hand. "Thanks for the invitation."

Short, balding and with a penchant for bright colors, the man had to be older than Eric's father, yet he sported a diamond stud in his left earlobe. "Thanks for the invitation," he mimicked, laughing. "Can you believe this guy?" Lawrence looked over at Dallas. "Modesty doesn't get you anywhere in this city. This man is a publicity genius. A little more arrogance is in order, don't you think?"

Dallas only smiled.

His gaze still fastened on Dallas, Lawrence took her hand. "Who do we have here?"

"This is Dallas." Annoyed that he couldn't even introduce her last name, Eric forced a smile. "And this is our host, Lawrence Horn."

"Pleased to meet you, Mr. Horn."

Lawrence raised her hand to his lips, his gaze staying on her face.

Amusement twinkled in Lawrence's pale blue eyes as he continued to study Dallas with an odd fascination. "Do I know you?" he finally asked.

She blinked and darted a nervous glance at Eric. "I don't believe we've ever met."

Lawrence squinted at her. "I know this face."

Eric didn't say a word. He was enjoying this way too much. Let her try to wiggle out of this one.

She shrugged a shoulder and casually withdrew her hand. "I guess we blondes all look alike."

Lawrence laughed heartily. "No, my dear, not all blondes are created equally."

A waiter appeared with a tray of canapés, and Dallas took an exceptionally long time to choose one of the morsels. Not that it mattered. Eric had faith in Horn. The guy was like a dog with a bone when he wanted something. And Dallas had clearly piqued his curiosity.

"I know." Lawrence nodded knowingly once the waiter had gone. "You're a model in Eric's ads. That's where I've seen you."

"No," Eric promptly offered. "She's never worked for me."

"Come now." Lawrence frowned. "It'll annoy me until I figure this out. You are a model, yes?"

Dallas chewed thoughtfully, and then said, "I used to model, but it's been quite a while."

"Hmm…" Lawrence shook his head, looking confused, and then started to say something further, but Dallas interrupted him.

She put a hand to her throat. "I'm sorry but—Eric, would you mind getting me something to drink?"

"Stay." Lawrence put his hand up to forestall Eric. With his other he snapped his fingers in the air and a waiter came running. That kind of behavior Eric despised. But Lawrence had other good qualities. Besides, he alone was responsible for about twenty percent of Webber and Thornton's revenue. And most of Eric's annual bonus.

They all gave the waiter their orders, and after he left, Lawrence said, "Please forgive my poor manners. I practically ambushed you at the door."

"Oh, please." Dallas put a hand on his arm. "We're

flattered that you personally greeted us. But I was wondering if it would be okay to wander into the gallery."

"Yes, of course." Lawrence waved expansively with his hand, the giant ruby he always wore on his ring finger flashing like wildfire under the lights. "No place is off limits to you, pretty lady." His mouth curving, he inclined his head toward Eric but kept his eyes on Dallas. "Talk him into buying you a piece of art. Always a good investment, in my estimation."

Eric snorted. As if he could afford anything in the building but a cigar.

Dallas laughed and then winked. "Maybe I'll buy *him* a piece of art."

Lawrence chuckled, clasping his hands together. "Such a delightful girl you are." Someone called to him and he briefly turned his head and waved. "Ah, I must go. But I will see you two later. Eric, she's a keeper." He smiled benignly at Dallas but again addressed Eric. "But I can see I don't have to tell you that."

"Odd character," Dallas said when Lawrence was out of earshot.

"Yeah, but he grows on you."

"I didn't mean odd in a bad way. I love interesting characters. People who don't fit the stereotype. Or don't try to mold themselves into an image to meet other people's expectations. I admire them." Her mouth twisted in a wry smile. "Even though he called me a girl."

Eric said nothing but studied her for a moment. Her expression and voice had changed. Subtly but enough that he noticed. Did people stereotype her? Is that why she was so guarded? Because of her looks, he easily saw how she could be misjudged. Truthfully, he'd pretty much done the same at first. But there was so much more depth to her. He'd only been allowed a glimpse so far, but he sensed the well was deep and he intended to dive in. Immerse himself.

The waiter brought their drinks—scotch for him and merlot for her—and then left to take Lawrence his apple martini. Eric recognized only a couple of people, who were busy talking to someone else, so he didn't feel as if he had to hang around and make small talk.

"Did you really want to go see the gallery?" he asked. "Or were you just trying to avoid the conversation?"

She smiled and took his hand. "Let's go see the gallery."

He followed her like a damn puppy dog. Hell, if she'd wanted to go to Siberia, he would've followed.

Like the building, the gallery was larger than it looked from the outside. Still, there were few paintings displayed, along with a ridiculous sculpture of what looked like a worm in the center of the room. As they passed it, he caught a glimpse of the fifty-thousand-dollar price tag and almost spit out his scotch.

She glanced over at him. "What's wrong?"

"Nothing."

"You don't really want to look at these paintings, do you?"

"I don't mind—" Chuckling, he shook his head. "Not even if they paid me."

She grinned. "Want to go back to the party?"

This time he took her hand, and pulled her close. "How about we go back to my place instead?"

Her eyes sparkled with promise. "I thought you'd never ask."

11

DALLAS MADE A DECISION. IF their relationship lasted for longer than a week, she'd tell him about herself. Everything. Well, not everything, but the stuff he needed to know. The part most important to him. That she wasn't a model or a socialite or something pretty to put on a pedestal. That she didn't have a power job and wasn't on the fast track at some Fortune 500 company.

The admission would probably end the relationship. No, it was an affair. Fantasy, really. But what did she expect? The whole thing started with a gag. For one night. She was the one who'd wanted to draw out the fantasy. Play dress up and pretend. And the sex. Oh, God, she got heated just thinking about the way he touched her, the way they moved together in perfect rhythm.

How did she know she'd actually start feeling something for him? That was the last thing she'd expected to happen. She didn't go for ambitious exec types. They reminded her too much of her father and brother.

She watched Eric unlock his apartment door, open it, reach inside to turn on a lamp and then stand aside for her to go in first. Yet he wasn't anything like her father or Cody. She doubted either one of them would give up

their precious time to help a struggling Chinese immi-
grant save his restaurant.

Maybe she was judging Eric too harshly. Maybe
what she did for a living wouldn't matter to him.

"Hey, what are you thinking so hard about?" He
pulled her in his arms as soon as they both got over the
threshold.

"Uh, are you going to close the door?"

"First things first." He covered her mouth with his
and kissed her so thoroughly, she literally couldn't
breathe.

With a light push to his chest she fell back laughing
and gasping at the same time. One of her heels caught in
the carpet, and when she missed a step, he caught her arm.

"How do you walk in those things?" He frowned at
her black stiletto heels, and then closed the door behind
him. "They look great but dangerous."

"Oh, they're lethal, all right. I'm lucky I haven't broken my neck."

"Why in the hell do women wear them? Not that I'm
complaining."

She shrugged. "It's the style, I guess. Why do you
guys wear baggy pants riding halfway down your butts?"

"Um, excuse me, but I don't think you'll ever see me
wearing baggy pants riding halfway down my ass."

She laughed. "Okay, and I don't think you'll be seeing me in stilettos much in the future."

Shrugging out of his jacket, he reared his head back,
feigning horror. "Wait a minute, I hope that's open for
discussion."

Smiling, she walked farther into the room and dropped her purse on a chair. "It used to be easy when I wore them all the time. Now, I have to admit, looking graceful or at least like I'm not teetering takes some maneuvering."

He tossed his jacket next to her purse. "What do you usually wear?"

"Boots."

"In the summer?"

"Yep."

"I've seen some killer heels on women's boots."

"Not the kind I wear," she said, watching him carefully. "Steel-toed work boots."

He laughed. "Really? Trying to start a new trend?"

"No, they're practical." *For work,* she almost added but stopped herself just in time. Perfect time to tell him. But she just couldn't do it. Not yet. It would ruin the evening. Ruin everything, probably.

At the end of the week, she promised herself, she'd explain. No, wrong. It wasn't about an explanation. She owed no such thing to anyone. She'd simply enlighten him. What he chose to do at that point was up to him.

She took a step closer, looking up at him, her smile purposeful as her gaze moved slowly to his mouth. "Why are we wasting time talking about boots?"

That's all it took. His eyes blazing, he pulled her against him, and just when she expected him to steal her breath away, he gently nibbled on the corner of her mouth and then lightly bit her lower lip. She closed her eyes and let her head loll back. With his tongue he traced her jaw to her earlobe, his touch so feathery light, she wasn't totally sure she wasn't imagining it.

"I take it these diamond earrings are real," he whispered, his warm breath penetrating her skin, and her nipples tightened in response.

"Yes." A graduation present from her parents, they were ridiculously expensive.

"Then I suggest you take them off." His tongue swirled around one of the diamonds, his breathing growing ragged. "Take everything off."

She smiled. "Is that an order?"

His mouth slowly curved against her skin. "It can be."

"Honey, if we were going to role-play, I'd be the general and you'd be the private."

"Want me to take my clothes off, ma'am?"

She laughed. "You're so easy."

He straightened and smiled at her. "Disgustingly easy, I know." He cupped her shoulder, wedging his fingers under the slim strap of her dress. Slowly he slid the fabric down and then he did the same with her other strap.

She undid his red silk tie, impatient when she had trouble with the knot, then pulled it from under his collar. He didn't try to help but just stared at her, the desire in his eyes so potent, it seemed to coat her skin like warm honey clinging to a biscuit.

When she tried to unbutton his shirt, he gently shoved her hands aside and reached around to unzip her dress. He pulled the zipper down halfway and then slipped his hands inside and stroked his palms down her bare skin to the curve of her buttocks.

Shivering, she moved closer so that she barely had room to unbutton his shirt. But she managed to free one button and then another. He massaged her lower back, his chest heavily rising and falling, and for a moment her hands stilled, her mind went blank. She closed her eyes.

Standing in his living room under the soft glow of the dimmed lamp, half undressed, his hands molding her back, was so intoxicating she actually felt light-headed and gripped his forearms.

"Dallas?"

Her lids felt so heavy, it was too much a struggle to lift them.

He moved his hand from her back and then tilted her chin up. "I wish you'd trust me," he whispered so huskily, it took her a moment to digest his words.

She opened her eyes. The sensual fog immediately lifted. "Why would you say that?"

"I want to keep seeing you."

She knew where he was going with this but she wasn't ready for that discussion. "I'd like that."

He smiled. "I don't even have your phone number."

"No?" She undid two more buttons, leaving his shirt hanging open. Placing both hands against his chest, she lowered her head and kissed a spot just above his right nipple.

His body tensed beneath her palms.

"All right." She touched the tip of her tongue to his budding nipple.

He sucked in a breath. "All right what?"

"I'll give you my number."

He moved just out of her reach. "And your last name?"

She pushed the shirt off his shoulder. His cuffs were still buttoned. Before she could unfasten them, he slid her dress down to her waist, leaving her breasts bare.

"What's your last name, Dallas?" His gaze stayed on her breasts. He touched one pearled nipple with the tip of his finger.

She got a hold of his cuff and slipped the button free. "Why is that so important?"

"Why is it so important to keep it from me?" He lowered his head and touched the same nipple with the tip of his tongue.

She freed the other cuff and pushed his shirt off. It fell to the floor. She went for his buckle, but he pulled away.

He smiled and slid her zipper the rest of the way down. Her dress joined his shirt on the floor, leaving her in nothing but a black thong and the stilettos.

"Answer me," he said softly, his gaze hungrily taking in her breasts, his nostrils flaring when he got to the small silk triangle at the juncture of her thighs.

Surely he could see her heart pounding. It felt as if it were going to burst through her skin. She held her breath and willed herself to keep from crying out as he cupped the weight of her breasts in each hand, using his thumbs to tease her nipples.

"Dallas?"

She couldn't blame him for coercing her like this. She'd done the same thing to him trying to avoid the conversation. But it didn't matter. Not really. Her last name wouldn't mean anything to him. She wasn't even listed in the phone book. None of her family was. "It's Shea."

"Dallas Shea. I like it."

He abandoned her breasts to slide his arms around her. Filling his palms with her bottom, his fingers lightly digging into her fleshy cheeks, he drew her against him. The friction of her nipples rubbing his chest hair raised goose bumps on her arms.

"Take off your pants," she said and kicked off one of her heels.

"Leave them on, okay?" One side of his mouth hiked up. "Just until we get in bed."

She tried to hold back a smile. "Is that where we're going?"

"I don't know. This is pretty thick carpet. Might be interesting to stay right here."

She slid her foot back into the shoe. No matter how soft the carpet, the idea of rubbing her bare bottom on it held no appeal.

As if he'd read her mind, he ran his palms down her backside. "Although I'd hate to see anything happen to this. Your skin is so incredibly soft. Like a baby's."

"The bed totally gets my vote." She didn't wait for him but jerked free his buckle.

"Impatient little thing." Grinning, he undid his buttons and fly.

"*Au contraire.* I think I've been very patient." She shoved his slacks down his hips, and he took it from there, yanking them off the rest of the way and throwing them in the direction of the couch.

He wore boxers again, his sex straining so hard against the tan silky fabric that she could see the outline of the head. She touched him there, swirling the tip of her finger until he shuddered. He cupped her shoulders as she hooked her fingers in his elastic waistband and drew the boxers down his legs.

On her way down she flicked her tongue across the velvety tip. He jerked, his fingers digging into her shoulders. But she had him trapped and she took her time ridding him of the boxers as she explored him with her tongue.

Moaning, he closed his eyes and threaded his fingers through her hair. Bobby pins bounced off her bare shoulders as they fell from the French twist she'd painstakingly created earlier. Her hair fell down her back, and he wove his fingers tighter through the strands as she drew the entire tip into her mouth.

His entire body shuddered. She took in more of him, teasing him with her swirling tongue until she reached the base. He moaned loudly, his fingers digging deeper, more painfully into her skin. With a jerk he pushed her back and then pulled her upright, startling her.

"Eric, what's—"

He shook his head, his eyes glassy. He couldn't seem to speak. He guided her backward until she met the couch and gently laid her down. And then not so gently pulled off her thong.

He kissed the top of her foot, worked his way to her knee and then spread her thighs. The reflex to squeeze them together was almost too great, and she balled her fists, closed her eyes and held her breath. Nothing happened for a moment and she knew he was looking at her. There. In the most intimate place.

She opened her eyes just as he lowered his head and kissed her nether lips. Then he spread them and slid his tongue inside. She nearly came off the couch. Realizing she still had her heels on, she struggled to kick them off before she tore the couch.

The movement seemed to arouse him further, and he used his tongue and fingers with such a fever, she knew it would all be over for her in seconds. She fisted his hair, trying to get him to slow down, but he continued, his tongue unrelenting, until the spasms started to rock her body.

Heat seared her and she cried out. Tears seeped from her eyes. She let go of his hair when she realized she was pulling it and then grabbed the armrest behind her head. He reached up to knead her breast, but he wouldn't stop the sensual assault of his mouth until she shifted her hips and squeezed her thighs together.

Without missing a beat he moved up to her breasts, teasing the nipple of one and then moving to the other and sucking it into his mouth. When he tried to slide his hand between her thighs, she pushed him away.

He raised his head in surprise. His face was slightly flushed, his darkened eyes hooded, his moist lips parted in confusion. She wanted to explain that nothing was wrong, that she only wanted to participate, but she could barely breathe. Instead she reached for him, and he smiled, shifting to give her better access.

It wasn't enough. The couch was too narrow to accommodate both of them, and she pushed herself upright to better maneuver. Like a starving man, he cupped her breasts and began suckling them feverishly, almost as if he couldn't get enough of her.

"Eric?"

He raised his head and captured her lips before she could say anything further. His enthusiasm was heady stuff, but she wanted to taste him, too.

She broke away, gasping for air. "Let's go to the bedroom."

He nodded. "Protection," he said unevenly. "In my nightstand."

She sensed he was about to start in again and she quickly left the couch.

He caught her hand, but she snatched it back.

"Oh, no you don't." She laughed at the wounded look he gave her. "Come on, or we'll never make it to the bedroom."

"We will. Eventually."

About to say they didn't have all night, she stopped herself. The truth was she had no intention of spending the night. But she didn't want to get into that conversation either.

"Well, I'm headed that way," she said over her shoulder and caught him staring at her backside. "Come if you want."

A cocky grin curved his mouth. "I have every intention of coming."

"I'm sure you do. So I suggest—" She let out a yelp when he leaped up and sprinted after her.

She ran to the bedroom, barely making it to the door-way when he wrapped his arms around her and dragged her to the bed. They both fell unceremoniously atop the rust-colored quilt.

"Thought you'd start without me, did you?" he murmured against her neck between kisses.

His slightly rough chin tickled, and she giggled. "It never crossed my mind."

"Not once?"

"Not even for a nanosecond."

"I don't know. You sounded like you enjoyed your own company last night."

She gasped and glared at him, hoping like hell she hadn't turned every shade of red. "You—you butthead."

He grinned. "Butthead, huh?"

"As if you didn't get *your* rocks off." She'd really hoped he wouldn't bring up last night. At the time she'd been so turned on, she hadn't cared about the prover-bial morning after. But even as she'd gotten dressed earlier for the reception, several flashbacks had had her cringing.

Eric laughed. "Hey, no denying it here. I think we should do that every night. That we're not together, that is," he said, taking a nip at her earlobe.

She bit her lip. Who knew how much longer that would be? A good reason to quit talking and get down to business, she decided and trailed her finger over the tip of his penis, spreading the thick drop of moisture she found there.

That got his attention. He sucked in a breath and

leaned back. She lowered her head and drew him into her mouth, flicking her tongue over the ridge she knew was especially sensitive. His thigh muscles tightened beneath her palms and his moan came out a strangled cry.

"Wait," he said, his breathing labored.

She shook her head and sucked him in deeper.

"Dallas. Please."

She smiled and ignored him.

"Dallas."

She had no intention of stopping, and he must have gotten it because he lay back and moaned, his thigh muscles bunching beneath her right hand. He was so big and hard, she had trouble manipulating him with her tongue, but that didn't seem to faze him. He threaded his fingers through her hair as his entire body shuddered and he cried out her name.

Never had she experienced such a rush of power and excitement. And satisfaction. Contentment. The whole thing scared her to death. This was only supposed to be about sex. Fulfilling a fantasy. She wasn't supposed to want to crawl inside him and stay forever.

12

"YO, DALLAS, YOU READY FOR lunch?" Tony stood on the scaffolding two stories above her, clearly not giving a damn that all the other guys heard him cavorting with the enemy. God bless him.

She shaded her eyes to look up at him. "Give me ten minutes, okay?"

"No problem. It'll probably take me that long to clean up Buddy's mess."

"Screw you, St. Angelo." Buddy threw down his work gloves and grabbed his lunch pail.

"Have a nice lunch," Tony called after him. "Don't hurry back."

Several feet away from Dallas the new guy doing the finishing work on the lobby banister started laughing. Nobody else did. At least not out loud. Most of them at one time or another had been the target of Buddy's vicious temper.

Not Tony, though. For some reason Buddy steered clear of him, even though Tony sometimes goaded him mercilessly. No one knew why, and Tony wouldn't say. The funny thing was everyone figured Buddy had some connection to either one of the higher-ups or the union bosses. His work was sloppy and his attendance poor. He should have been fired years ago.

That's the kind of thing that really infuriated Dallas. Most of the women she knew worked twice as hard so they weren't singled out. And then jerks like Buddy skated by for years.

Yesterday and today had been good days. No traffic duty, and Dallas had gotten to work indoors. It helped, too, that she spent most of the time daydreaming of Eric. Twice she'd had to jerk herself back to reality to keep from sanding off the rest of her pathetically short fingernails.

For the first time, she'd forgotten to bring her work gloves. Hardly a surprise considering she hadn't gotten home until four in the morning. Amazing she wasn't a wreck. Sure made concentration difficult.

"Ready?"

She looked up at Tony. "Has it been ten minutes already?"

"Twelve, and I'm starving." He handed her *Aladdin* lunch pail to her and inclined his head toward the unfinished railing she'd been sanding. "This will be here when you get back."

She sighed. "Much to my delight."

"Where are your gloves?"

"I forgot them."

He frowned at her hands. "You should keep a spare in your lunch pail. I have one but it won't fit you. Especially not for this kind of close work."

"Not a big deal," she said, shrugging and heading toward the door that led to the park where they always ate. Well, not really a park—more a triangle of grass with two trees and a couple of benches where mothers stopped with their strollers to chat over a cup of coffee.

Tony followed, saying nothing, until they got to the park and sat on the grass under a pine tree. Then he took one of her hands and inspected it. Lots of skin tears, and two knuckles on her right hand were scraped and bleeding a little.

She winced. Damn it. They looked like hell, and it was a big deal. Eric would... She put the brakes on her wayward thoughts. This wasn't about Eric. If he wanted someone more glamorous, that was his problem. She couldn't mold herself according to someone else's plan.

But her nails and hands did look like hell.

"Hey."

She looked at Tony.

He smiled. "It's okay to be a girl, you know. I actually like them."

"Don't be a wiseass. This isn't about that."

He removed his hard hat and raked his fingers through his dark wavy hair. "I've never asked you questions, right?"

"Oh, God."

"Relax. I'm not gonna get too personal."

"Good." She opened her lunch pail and got out the waterless hand wash.

He stared at her with an amused look on his face. "I had this neighbor in Queens. She moved in next door when I was about ten and she was maybe twelve or thirteen. Jenny was so damn cute. Long blond hair about your color. Blue eyes, too. And dimples..." He shook his head, smiling. "She wore her hair in braids all rolled up and tucked away because her mother wouldn't let her cut it. And she always had a baseball cap on. Never once saw her in a dress. I doubt she owned one."

He paused and stared at two kids playing ball. Tempted to tell him to shut up, Dallas took out a green apple and bit into the tart fruit. Obviously he was using the story as a parable because he thought it somehow applied to her. Which it clearly didn't.

"I wasn't interested in girls yet," he continued, "but some of the other guys in the neighborhood kept sniffing around her. She'd get so mad, she'd call them out to the park and threaten to whip their asses. If you treated her like one of the guys, she was fine. But if—"

"Tony?"

"Yeah?"

"Shut up and eat your lunch."

He laughed. "I'm just saying—"

"Don't, okay. Besides, you got it all wrong."

"Go ahead, straighten me out."

She sighed. "Why do you do this job?"

He snorted. "Why do you think? Number one, I hate wearing a suit and tie. Number two, I don't know how to do anything else."

"Don't give me that. How much money did you make off the last two brownstones you refurbished?"

He grinned, shrugged.

"That was a rhetorical question. I know damn well

you had to have made more than five years' salary working here." She sighed and put down her apple.

"So? Why you bustin' my chops all of a sudden? I'm on your side, remember?"

"I know. Really I do." She and Tony were a lot more alike than she'd thought, she just realized. Both restless. Both wanting something a little more but not ready to cave in or sell out.

He was much more ambitious than he'd ever admit. She was probably the only one who knew, but four years ago he'd bought a foreclosed brownstone, lived in it while he'd renovated it and then sold it for a hefty profit before moving on to the next one and starting over.

Shaking his head and frowning, he unwrapped his sandwich. "I think you need to get laid."

A strangled laugh escaped her and she punched his arm. If he only knew… "Now you sound just like the rest of them."

"That was low, Shea, really low."

"You asked for it." She stared at her half-eaten apple, tempted to tell Tony about Eric. But really, what kind of advice could Tony give her? Besides, then she'd have to confess her lie. No, not a lie. Her *pretense*. She winced. *Fantasy* had a better ring. Either way it sounded awful.

Besides, there was more on her mind than Eric lately. Like how tired she was getting of the job, of having to wash her hair three times every night to get the dust out. She'd made her point with her parents by now. And she'd paid off most of her debts and started saving some money. Maybe it was time to start looking for something else. Possibly even put her business degree to some use.

Of course, her restlessness had nothing to do with Eric and the fact that he most likely came from some upper-crust Philadelphia family who'd expected more of their son than to date a construction worker. Nor did it have anything to do with how much she'd been enjoying the dressing up and evenings out. It was just time to move on. That's all. Nothing more.

Tony grunted. "Quit with the long face. Let's move to neutral ground. Tell me about the meeting."

She looked blankly at him. "That was Tuesday."

"Yeah, so? We didn't talk yesterday. You skipped lunch so you could knock off early. Must have had a hot date or something."

She looked away. Hard to believe is was only Thursday. That meant she'd met Eric five days ago. That didn't seem possible. So much had happened. She felt so much more than she should. Feeling the weight of Tony's stare, she glanced over at him and mentally flinched at the fascinated curiosity in his eyes.

She cleared her throat. "That was only the second meeting. We have a long way to go. We didn't even have that good a turnout."

"They're afraid of losing their jobs. Can't blame them."

"I don't. Believe me."

"Yeah, I know. So what are you gonna do about it?"

"Me?"

He snorted. "Yeah, you. Who else has the smarts and the guts to get changes made?"

"I just want to get them to the point where they don't feel they have to take crap from anybody."

"And then?"

"I'm not their mother."

He smiled. "I'm just saying...you stirred the pot."

"That doesn't put me in charge. What they need to do is unify."

His eyebrows drew together in a thoughtful frown. "They still need a leader."

"God, you look like my father."

"Shit." He gave her a lopsided grin. "You're not gonna be able to walk away from this."

"Who said anything about walking away?" Guilt needled her. She wasn't exactly anxious to carry the torch. She wasn't even sure she wanted to organize another meeting.

"Well, butter my toast. Aren't you getting testy?"

She laughed. "Butter my toast?"

Tony shrugged, looking adorably sheepish. "My mother's from the south," he muttered. "She says stuff like that sometimes."

"Who knew?"

"What?"

She shook her head. "Is she Italian?"

"Nope. Half French and half Irish. Atlanta born and bred."

"Wow! I always pictured you as part of this big Italian family who's been here for three generations."

"Stereotyping, huh?"

"No."

Tony grinned.

Her indignation died a quick death, and she sighed. "That did sound pretty bad."

"Nah, I just wanted to bust your chops. Anyway, you got it half right." Angling his head, he looked past her, the odd expression on his face making her turn to see what had captured his interest.

"Dakota?" She stared as her sister approached from not six feet away, clearly uncomfortable walking in heels on the soft grass. "What are you doing here?"

"Looking for you, obviously," she said, the sarcasm in her tone entirely uncharacteristic. She darted an unsmiling glance at Tony.

"Why?" Dallas pushed to her feet because she knew Dakota wasn't about to sit on the grass. Not that Dallas blamed her. The gorgeously tailored navy blue suit she wore hadn't simply been yanked off the rack. "How did you know I was here?"

"I stopped at your job site." The clipped tone and the annoyance in her gray eyes pretty much said it all. "How can you work with those Neanderthals?"

Tony started laughing, and Dakota gave him a scathing look. "This is when you're supposed to say 'present company excepted,'" he said, dusting his hands together and getting to his feet.

Dakota's perfectly arched eyebrows went up. She wanted to say something. Dallas knew that look. But Dakota was the genteel one of the siblings. She needed harmony even if it meant trying to please everyone.

Tony gave her one of his killer grins. "You have to be the sister."

Dakota didn't seem as susceptible as most women were to Tony's smile, and Dallas quickly made the introduction before Tony did or said something totally annoying. Dakota grudgingly extended her hand, and Tony made a show of wiping his palms down the front of his jeans. Which would've been okay if his jeans were clean.

Dallas sighed. Designer suit, perfect nails, perfect hair, perfect everything, her sister was just the kind of woman Tony liked to give a hard time. At the risk of seeming rude, she gave Tony her back and asked, "So, what's up?"

"I wanted to remind you about dinner at Mother and Dad's Saturday night."

"You came in person for that?"

"Yes, because it's that important."

Dallas glanced over her shoulder at Tony. He'd taken the hint, sat down and returned to his lunch. His gaze, however, stayed on Dakota. Poor guy. That was never going to happen.

"Why is it so important?"

"Because you didn't show up the last two times."

"Wrong terminology. I didn't *not* show up. I declined the invitation. Big difference."

"You know what I mean."

Dallas groaned. She hadn't really thought about dinner yet. "I'll be there, okay?"

"Promise?"

"Yes."

Dakota grinned. "Want me to pick you up?"

"Don't you trust me?" She smiled back. "No, thanks, I don't need a ride." A wild thought popped into her head. "Hey, are you taking a date?"

Dakota's eyes widened. "To Mother and Dad's? I—I hadn't even considered it." Her gaze narrowed, and she shot a look at Tony. "Are you?"

Dallas bit back a laugh. Her sister could pontificate all she wanted about the importance of family and the duty of children to their parents, but when it came right down to it, she kept her distance, too. Not as blatantly as Dallas, but she wasn't exactly ready to open the door to her life.

"Oh, I don't know," Dallas said slowly. "I'm thinking about it."

Dakota blinked, and her gaze briefly flitted to Tony again.

"Not him. He's just a friend." Dallas smiled. "But I could bring him for you if you like."

"Are you—" Dakota lowered her voice. Fortunately a couple of kids arguing over a ball drowned her out. "Are you insane?"

"Why? He's really a nice guy."

With a haughty lift of her chin, Dakota adjusted her starched white collar. "Dinner will be served at seven. Mother says to come anytime after six. And I suggest you warn her if you do bring someone else."

"Thank you. I never would have thought of that."

Dakota rolled her eyes. "See you Saturday," she said as she turned and headed for the sidewalk.

Dallas idly watched her go, wondering why in the hell she'd even given the idea of taking Eric a passing thought. Of course, she hadn't, really. Mostly she'd wanted to tease Dakota.

"Hey, how come she didn't say goodbye?"

At the sound of Tony's voice behind her, Dallas smiled and went back to join him.

With an exaggerated sigh he put a hand to his heart. "I think I'm in love."

"You said that on Monday about the blonde at the deli."

"Did I?" He frowned. "Hmm."

She shook her head, chuckling as she reclaimed her spot on the grass and unwrapped a piece of Gouda. She probably ought to set him straight. Not that she thought he was really serious. Or not that she wouldn't like to see them hook up. Tony would be good for Dakota. He'd loosen her up. But she'd never go for someone like him. Not in a million years.

Tony grinned suddenly, his gaze focused on something in the distance, and he lifted his hand in a wave.

Dallas twisted around in time to see Dakota snub him and disappear around the corner.

"She turned for a last look," Tony said, still grinning. "She likes me."

"You're too much."

"That's what all the women say."

"Oh, please." Dallas laughed, darted another look in the direction her sister had gone. Dakota was not the type to look back. Interesting.

She was about to take a bite of cheese when her cell phone rang. As she pulled it off the clip on her belt, she checked caller ID. Her heart skipped two beats. It was Eric.

"Hello?"

"Hey. It's me," he said. "Tell me you haven't had lunch yet."

"Just had it." Giving Tony an apologetic look, she struggled to her feet.

Snorting, he tore open a bag of chips. "Nice having lunch with you."

She glared at him before moving out of earshot.

"Uh, sorry." Eric cleared his throat. "Sounds like I've interrupted."

"No, not really. That was one of the guys I work with."

"Ah, well, since you already had lunch, how about a drink after work?"

She glanced down at her miserable-looking nails. "What time?"

"I'm flexible."

"Okay, well…" Her gaze on her watch, she started calculating the time it would take her to dash home and get cleaned up.

Several feet from Dallas one of the kids playing ball let out an ear-piercing scream.

"What was that?"

"Some kid." She walked farther away as the fight between the little boys escalated.

"Where are you?"

"In a park."

"You ate lunch there?"

"Yeah."

Silence stretched and she knew what he was thinking. A park was a strange place to have lunch with a business associate. God, she didn't want Eric to think she was jerking him around.

"Okay, well, if you're busy, no problem," he said, his tone suddenly and achingly indifferent.

"No, really I'm not. I'd met my sister here. She left a minute before you called."

"Ah, I didn't know she worked in the city."

"Yep. Not far from here."

"Where's here?"

Dallas smiled. "Where should we meet for a drink?"

He sighed, his impatience with her evasiveness clear. "Any preference?"

"How about— Oh, no!"

"What?"

"I can't tonight. I'm meeting Wendy and Trudie." How could she have forgotten? "My roommate and another college friend. We get together once a month. Tonight's it." Why did she feel compelled to give him an explanation? She didn't owe him any. "Sorry."

He hesitated for a long tense moment. "Is everything okay with us?"

"Yes. Absolutely."

Tony approached carrying both their lunch pails. He pointed to his watch, she nodded and he headed back toward the job site. They had five minutes to clock back in. She couldn't be late.

"Still there?" she asked, starting after Tony but keeping a safe distance so that he couldn't hear her conversation.

"Yeah, how about tomorrow night then? Have you

seen *Aida?* I think I can get decent tickets, and then we could have dinner afterward...."

She cringed. "I can't."

"Okay," he said slowly.

"I promised a friend I'd help her move out of her apartment. Tomorrow evening is the only time we can do it so she can be out by Saturday."

"Need a strong back?"

"Who? You?"

"Very funny."

She stopped several yards outside the door so he couldn't hear the buzz of electric saws and drills as she scrambled for something to say that wouldn't put him off. He couldn't meet Nancy. Tony was going to be there, too. Eric couldn't meet any of them. Not yet.

She swallowed hard, hoping she wasn't about to make the biggest mistake of her life. "How about Saturday? Want to go to dinner at my parents' house?"

13

ERIC HUNG UP THE RECEIVER and then stared at the phone. They'd been going out for one week and he'd agreed to have dinner with her parents. This whole thing with Dallas could hardly get more bizarre. One minute he thought she was brushing him off, and the next she was asking him to meet her family. Not just her parents but her brother and sister—they were all going to be there. Was he ready for this?

"Hey." Tom strolled into his office. "You going out today or eating in?"

"What?"

"Lunch." Tom frowned. "What's the matter with you?"

Eric picked up a paper clip and absently twirled it around his fingers. "She asked me to go to her parents' house for dinner."

"Who?"

Eric blinked at him. "Dallas."

Tom sank into the chair opposite Eric and stared. "You're still seeing her?"

"I took her to Horn's reception last night."

"No shit."

"So?"

Tom snorted. "Unbelievable. This is serious."

"No, it's not."

"Dinner with her parents? Right."

"It's not like that." Eric got up to get a cup of coffee.

"This means you must have boinked her already, right?"

"You asshole. Get out."

"Whoa!" Tom laughed and got up to follow Eric down the hall to the coffee room. "This is serious."

Too late Eric realized he should never have said anything to Tom. Except how would Eric know he'd receive such a juvenile reaction? They'd never had a serious conversation about a woman in his life. Hell, there never had been anyone with whom Eric had considered having a serious relationship.

He made sure no one else was in the coffee room and then turned to Tom and in a low voice said, "Okay, this may be going somewhere, so you gotta lay off."

Tom's eyes met Eric's and the laughter disappeared. Surprise flickered and then genuine concern. "Sure. I get it."

"Good." Eric got his coffee and headed back to his office, hoping like hell Tom didn't follow. He didn't expect his friend to give him a hard time, but he didn't want to field any more questions either. Questions that would expose the embarrassing fact that Dallas had revealed so little about herself.

He got back to his office, and sure enough, right behind him was Tom. Sighing, Eric sat down. "By the way, I'm eating in today. I have a couple of important calls to make."

Tom hovered in the doorway, a dozen questions in his eyes. "Anyone picking up a sandwich for you?"

"I'm having it delivered." Eric picked up his phone receiver for added effect.

"All right, tomorrow maybe."

"Sure. We'll go over to Pete's for a Philly cheesesteak."

"You got it." Tom checked his watch. "Better go. I've got a meeting in an hour."

"See ya later." Watching with relief as Tom headed for the lobby elevators, Eric replaced the receiver. He picked up his coffee and took a sip. Today he'd skip lunch. He wasn't really hungry. If he wanted it later, he had a Snickers stashed in his desk somewhere.

The phone rang, and he muttered a curse when the sound startled him into sloshing coffee onto an expense report. He grabbed the receiver. Before he could greet the caller, Lawrence Horn walked into his office.

"I wanted to give you a heads-up," the receptionist said over the phone line. "Mr. Horn is on his way to your office right now."

"Thanks," Eric muttered and hung up.

"Poor girl, she did try to stop me," Lawrence said as he sank into the chair Tom had vacated.

Eric didn't even try to feign innocence. "What are you doing roaming around this side of town?"

"Oh, I thought I'd slum for a while." Today he wore a royal-blue suit, cream-colored shirt and black tie. "See how the other half lives."

Used to his harmless sense of humor, Eric paid no

attention to the obnoxious remark. "Great party last night. Thanks again."

"You left early." Lawrence wagged a finger and grinned. "Although I can certainly understand why. She's exquisite. Truly exquisite. I applaud you."

Eric snorted, glad Dallas wasn't here to hear that. "Wish I could take credit."

"Oh, was I being politically incorrect?" Lawrence frowned thoughtfully, and then a sly smile curved his mouth. "You'll both forgive me when you hear my offer."

"Offer? What offer?"

"I want you to design an ad campaign around her."

"For what?"

"I don't know." Lawrence waved an impatient hand. "Her face haunted me all night. I even dreamed about her. Surely you can use her to link my companies or something. After all, Revlon and L'Oreal have models as spokeswomen or what have you."

"They're cosmetic companies. Of course they would use—"

"Oh, you sound like Bruce." Lawrence muttered an expletive. "You're supposed to be creative. Think of something."

Eric shook his head. "She doesn't model any more." Actually he didn't even know if that was true. He didn't know anything about her.

"She will." Lawrence stood and daintily dusted off his lapels with his manicured fingertips. "Money always talks. For her and you." He smiled. "I guess I'll stop by the old man's office on my way out. Haven't seen him in ages."

Eric recognized the veiled threat. Lawrence was going to fill Webber in. If Eric didn't produce, Webber would be all over him.

Then again, maybe he was getting worked up for nothing. Maybe Dallas would be open to a modeling contract. Especially if the price was right. It still galled him that he knew so little about her. But that would change. Saturday night. She was finally going to let him into her private sanctum. Suddenly Saturday couldn't come fast enough.

"YOU HAVE A DEATH WISH. YOU know that, right?" Wendy grabbed a handful of peanuts from the glass bowl the cocktail server had set on their table.

Trudie stopped sipping her margarita long enough to make a face at Wendy. "Why are you so negative?"

"Oh, please. Once he meets her parents, you don't think they'll be history?"

Dallas sighed, beginning to wish she hadn't brought up the subject. "I think Wendy's on to something. Maybe I do have a death wish."

Both women looked at her as if she'd just told them she was pregnant. Dallas causally glanced at the guy at the table to the right of her, so close he might as well have been sitting with them. The place was crowded, every table taken, people standing four deep at the bar. Even the poor cocktail servers had trouble squeezing in between the tables bulging with yuppies in suits and loosened ties. She would rather have gone somewhere else, but it had been Trudie's turn to choose the place.

Dallas leaned closer and spoke more softly. "I mean, maybe I want him to find out but I'm too chicken to actually tell him myself. Does that make sense?"

"Yeah, in a creepy Freudian sort of way." Wendy took a thoughtful sip of her club soda. She saved her calories for peanuts or any other snacks the bar offered.

Dallas did the opposite. Her calories generally went toward alcohol when she was out. Trudie, on the other hand, had no boundaries. She simply indulged in everything.

Trudie licked the salted rim of her glass and then put it down near the peanuts. "Well, kiddo, if you want him to find out, this will be one hell of a good way."

"Except I really don't want him to find out." Dallas sighed. "I don't think."

The other two exchanged sympathetic looks.

Wendy spoke first. "Okay, I hate to point out the obvious, but once you take him to meet the parents, it's gonna be out of your hands."

"First, this isn't about meeting my parents. Second, they rarely talk about anything but themselves and whatever research they're currently involved in, and when they don't have the floor, my brother does. Since they dismiss my job out of hand, they never ask about it. In fact, I think they like to pretend it doesn't exist."

Wendy reached for another handful of peanuts. "Yeah, but you don't think they'll be a little more chatty about you with a new face at the table?"

"Not if I warn my mother ahead of time."

They both chuckled, and then Trudie said, "Like she's going to listen to you."

"She will. Otherwise she knows I won't be showing up for any more—" Dallas hooked two sets of fingers in the air "—quote 'family dinners.'"

"Ah, blackmail," Wendy said, nodding. "Good move."

Trudie frowned, clearly not buying the plan. "What about your father or brother? Or even Dakota, for that matter?"

"Dakota will be totally cool. Mother will take care of Cody and my father."

"I still think it's risky." Wendy signaled the waitress for another club soda. "But, of course, I vote you just tell him. If he doesn't like it, screw him. You don't need that. You guys want another one?"

They both nodded, and Wendy took care of it with a few hand signals to the waitress.

"I don't know," Trudie said. "I just don't think she should be hasty. Once he knows her better, he may be more forgiving."

"Oh, jeez," Wendy said loudly enough to earn her a couple of glares. "Like Dallas needs forgiveness. How would you like it if some guy told you he didn't want you working at a department store?"

"That's not what I meant. You always choose to take everything I say wrong." Trudie got that huffy look on her face that meant the silent treatment wasn't far behind. Which also meant it was time to call it a night.

Dallas sighed. "I think Trudie was talking about me playing a mind game with him. The whole mystery thing."

"Exactly." Trudie sat back, her arms folded across her chest.

"Whatever." Wendy fished the lime out of her drink and popped it into her mouth.

Dallas winced. She liked the flavor of lime, but the actual fruit? Eew. "So, what's happening with you, Trudie? Your boss has to love that display window. It really is something."

Trudie's entire expression changed. "They think I'm a genius."

"You are. Wendy, you should go by and see the window. Totally awesome."

The conversation went in a neutral direction and everyone seemed to relax. Pretty typical girls' night out for them, actually. Dallas didn't know why she insisted on throwing Wendy and Trudie together. They were so different. But both dear friends, and maybe she was more like Dakota than she cared to admit.

Dallas liked harmony, the scales perfectly balanced. It was the Libra in her. That's why she couldn't grasp why she'd set herself up as she had. Saturday could be disastrous. And totally avoidable. It wasn't too late to back out. She had to really think about this. As if she hadn't wrung herself out worrying already.

She took a deep breath, trying to stay focused on the conversation. But something kept niggling at her, something too horrible to admit. There was possibly another reason she wanted to take Eric to dinner at her parents'.

His meeting them, seeing the beautiful white Victorian in which she'd grown up, would legitimize her.

Prove she was more than a construction worker. That she was his kind of woman. And no matter how much she rejected the possibility, it sat heavily in her stomach, eating at her, making her sick. Because if it were true, that would make her a snob just like them.

ERIC OPENED THE DOOR TO HIS apartment, his eyes lighting with appreciation. "You look beautiful."

"Thank you." She hadn't even made it over the threshold before he pulled her into his arms and kissed her. She sighed. "Maybe we should stay here."

"Tempting." He smiled and leaned back to look at her. "But I don't want to disappoint your parents. That wouldn't put us off to a very good start."

She stifled a nervous laugh. Start? Tonight could be the finish. "You really don't have to wear a tie, you know."

He stepped back and studied the obscenely expensive red silk blouse she'd received as a Christmas present from her parents but would never have spent the money on herself. With it she wore casual cream-colored slacks and taupe flats.

"Okay." He loosened the conservative gray tie and then pulled it off. "Better?"

"You don't even have to wear a sports jacket."

He looked doubtful. "What will your father and brother be wearing?"

She laughed. "You sound like a twelve-year-old girl."

"What?" One eyebrow went up. "A twelve-year-old girl, huh?"

She backed up. "Yep."

"Better take it back."

"Or else?"

He grabbed her, and she came up against his chest, laughing, struggling for a breath. She tilted her head back, anticipating his kiss, but he only touched the corner of her mouth lightly with the tip of his tongue.

"Hey." She raised herself on her tiptoes.

A cocky grin curved his lips. "Hey, what?"

"You don't want to play this game with me," she said sweetly. "You'll lose."

"What game?" He grunted when she rubbed against his fly and then quickly retreated. "You're a cruel woman."

"Uh-huh."

"Not even going to deny it, huh?"

"Nope." She smiled and rubbed up against him again. He was hard already.

His eyes closed briefly and he moaned. "You're damn lucky the car is going to be here in ten minutes."

"I don't know why you hired one. We could have taken the train."

"I don't understand why you wouldn't let me pick you up at your apartment."

She stiffened and stepped around him to smooth her hair. Her blouse had come loose in the back, and she took her time tucking it in.

"Dallas, I'm not trying to give you a hard time. I figured that going to your parents' meant the mystery stuff was over."

"I was already in the neighborhood." She shrugged,

finding it difficult to meet his eyes while she was lying. "It just seemed easier to meet you here. You still have time to change if you want to wear something more comfortable."

He hesitated, staring at her as if deciding whether to push the issue. Finally he said, "Such as?"

"Jeans, if you want."

"Jeans?"

"Sure."

He cast a skeptical glance at her slacks. "I'll pass on the jeans, but I will lose the jacket."

"That works. Here." She slipped around him to help take off his jacket, and he caught her wrist.

"Anxious to undress me?"

"Always." She smiled, freeing herself so she could stow the jacket on the couch without wrinkling it.

Eric followed her. "The hell with the driver. He can wait."

She put up a restraining hand. "Down boy. Seriously. We need to get through this dinner first."

His gaze narrowed. "That doesn't sound encouraging. Is there something I should know about tonight?"

"Nothing, really." Dallas sighed, wondering how much to say without spooking him. She'd already had a talk with her mother, warning her that playing old tapes would not be welcome. If the conversation went in the direction of her job or personal life, Dallas would promptly leave. "My parents can be a bit trying, though."

"Trying," he repeated warily.

"A couple of pains in the ass, actually." She smiled. "But don't worry. They'll be on their best behavior with you."

He frowned, looking worried, and she was sorry she'd said anything. "Define *pains*," he said.

She took his hand and squeezed it. "You'll probably find them quite charming. It's me. We haven't always seen eye to eye on things. And I haven't been what you call a dutiful daughter."

"Ah, I get it." He seemed to relax. "Will I like your brother and sister?"

"Dakota will charm your socks off. Cody will talk business and about the stock market until your eyes glaze over. They're both lawyers."

"What about your parents?"

"Dad's a judge and Mother is a biology professor."

"Whoa." Eric looked more than a little surprised. "Well-educated family."

"Yep." And then there was her, the black sheep of the family. The thorn in the otherwise perfect rose.

"You should be proud of them."

"I am."

He smiled, disbelief flickering in his eyes, but he wisely kept his own counsel.

The thing was she really was proud of them. They'd all made enormous contributions to society. Well, her father and Dakota particularly. Her sister tirelessly worked pro bono cases on behalf of battered women, and her father had been responsible for groundbreaking legislation protecting abused children.

Her mother and Cody were more mercenary and strived to make the society columns. Social status was important, and they didn't stray from their ivory towers. But they were basically good people and did their jobs well. Dallas had no problem with their choices in life. None of her business, really. She just wished they stayed out of hers.

She sighed. "I know I've given you the wrong impression. I love my family." She shrugged. "We're just different. It's hard to explain."

A thoughtful frown drew his eyebrows together, and he looked at her as if he weren't really seeing her. "I get it." He blinked. "It's the same with me and my family."

She smiled, doubtful he truly understood, but that was okay.

The buzzer rang from the lobby, signaling that their driver had arrived. This was it. No turning back now. Within forty minutes they'd be in Tarrytown.

Dallas took a deep breath. "Okay. Showtime."

14

ERIC LAUGHED HUMORLESSLY TO himself as they passed through the double white iron gates that allowed them onto the Shea property. Not considered an estate—at least not by Tarrytown standards—but damn close. About an acre of sloping green lawn, large old pine and oak trees and a curving driveway that led to a stately white Victorian that had to be a hundred years old. Nope, this wasn't the same at all.

If Dallas were to see the place where he grew up, her jaw would hit the ground. His parents still lived there. In a small three-bedroom row house where if you sat on the porch, all you could see was thick black smoke rising from the steel mill where nearly everyone in town worked, including his father and brothers. God, was he glad to be away from there.

When his pop had retired last year, Eric had tried to get them to move, offered to subsidize the cost after they sold the house, but they wouldn't hear of it. That was home. They were happy. Eric couldn't understand that mentality. But he did respect it and had backed off.

He looked over at Dallas. She'd lain her head back

against the leather seat, and idly stared out the window. "You grew up here?"

"What?" She brought her head up. "Oh, yeah."

"Nice. Very nice."

"The house has been in the family for four generations. My father inherited it from my grandparents when I was about three. Before that we lived in the city." She smiled. "Obviously I don't remember. This has always been home to me."

"I don't think I've seen this much grass in two years. You must miss living out here."

She smiled. "How quickly you've forgotten our ride in Central Park."

"Oh, no." He squeezed her hand and their gazes met and held. "I haven't forgotten."

The car came to a stop. The driver had pulled into the circular drive that put them close to the front door. He got out, dressed in a white dress shirt, black slacks, his graying wavy hair slicked back, and opened Dallas's door.

Totally juvenile, he knew, but Eric hoped her family was watching. First impressions were important. He didn't want them to think their daughter had come with some bum from Pittsburgh.

After they both got out, the driver, in accented English, asked what time they wanted to be picked up. Eric looked at Dallas.

She shrugged. "Ten minutes?"

The driver frowned.

Eric laughed. "She's joking." He glanced at his watch. Stupid, since he knew what time it was. Maybe he was a little nervous. "How about nine-thirty? Does that sound about right?"

Dallas nodded. "Fine."

The driver got back in the car, and they started up the front steps. Before they got to the door, it opened. A short dark-haired woman of indeterminate age, dressed all in black, stood at the threshold smiling.

"Tilly." Dallas took the last two steps at once and hugged the slight woman. "It's been so long since I've seen you."

"That's because you don't come to visit your parents often enough," the woman scolded with gruff affection. She stepped back, holding Dallas by the shoulders to look at her. "You've gained some weight."

"Uh, thanks for pointing that out." Dallas glanced over at him, a touch of pink in her cheeks.

"It's good. You were too thin." The woman squeezed Dallas's upper arm. "Give me another hug."

Dallas obliged her and then turned to Eric. "This is Tilly. She's been with us forever."

Tilly extended her hand. Her palm was slightly rough. "I'm the Sheas' housekeeper."

"I'm Eric," he said when it seemed Dallas had forgotten to finish the introduction.

"Sorry." Dallas briefly covered her mouth with her hand to stifle a giggle. She sounded like a little girl.

Tilly apparently noticed, too, and snorted. "I used to be the children's nanny, as well. Sometimes I think they haven't grown up yet."

"I haven't." Dallas tossed her hair back and shooed Tilly inside. "Where is everyone?"

"On the back patio having drinks and watching the sunset."

Eric sighed. So much for the grand entrance complete with car and driver. He followed the two women through the large foyer, catching glimpses of the dining room on the right and the living room on the left. Lots of polished hardwood floors and Persian rugs, large vases of fresh flowers, an eclectic array of art pieces, no doubt expensive, in unexpected places.

They came to a sunroom, and beyond the French doors he saw them—three women and two men sitting around a glass table, looking casually chic with drinks in hand—and he suddenly wished like hell he hadn't let Dallas talk him out of bringing a bottle of wine.

Dallas abruptly stopped. "Who is that?"

"Clair Sumner." Tilly winked. "Your brother seems serious about this one."

Dallas crossed her arms and briefly hugged herself. She seemed unduly annoyed. Almost panicked, which made no sense. "Mother didn't tell me there would be someone else here besides family."

Tilly's brows came down in a perplexed frown. "Is that a problem?"

Dallas blinked at her and then darted a look at Eric. She turned back to Tilly with a forced smile. "No, of course not. It's just— Oh, God, please tell me she's not dull as dishwater."

"Shush." Tilly pinched her wrist. "Behave yourself, young lady."

"Ouch." She rubbed the assaulted area. "I'm not going to say anything." She leaned close to Eric and rolled her eyes. "He's had the most boring girlfriends you could possibly imagine."

Something had clearly spooked her. She'd tried to cover up her alarm, but he knew the woman's presence had somehow unnerved Dallas. Tilly seemed to know, as well.

An older woman with a remarkable resemblance to Dallas spotted them. She said something that made everyone turn around and watch him and Dallas go out the French doors. The two men stood.

"Before you start getting all chatty, tell me what you'd like to drink," Tilly said.

Eric glanced at the drinks on the table.

"We have just about everything," she said softly, her kind dark eyes putting him at ease.

"Scotch?"

She nodded.

"Thanks."

"He likes it neat," Dallas said. "And I'll have—"

"I know what you want." Laughing, Tilly shook her head and closed the doors.

Dallas cleared her throat and moved toward the others. "Hi, everyone, I'd like you to meet Eric Harmon."

Lean and tall and looking remarkably fit, the older man, who had to be Dallas's father, gave him a warm smile and a firm handshake. His hair was almost entirely white, yet he didn't even look sixty. "Harrison Shea," he said. Dallas's father, of course.

"Pleased to meet you, sir," Eric said, and was mildly amused that the man didn't object to the *sir* part.

"That's my mother, Andrea." Dallas gestured with her hand, and the woman nodded, her smile not as warm as her husband's, her gaze definitely speculative.

"That's Dakota."

No doubt they were sisters. The same high cheekbones and heart-shaped face, but her hair was a darker blond and her eyes were more gray than blue. And like Dallas, she had a great smile.

"And this is my brother, Cody."

The man nodded, his lips barely moving. Eric didn't take it personally. This was the kind of guy who wasn't comfortable smiling. Dallas had warned him her brother was conservative. No kidding. One look said it all—the short haircut, the preppy white oxford shirt and khaki slacks, the serious gray eyes, no laugh lines there.

She looked at the woman next to him and smiled. "I understand you're Clair."

The brunette nodded and stood, petite, maybe five-two, a Lilliputian in a land of giants. Not a single Shea could be under five-eight.

They shook hands all the way around, Andrea the only one not getting to her feet. Which didn't bother him. Feeling like one of her biology experiments being viewed under a microscope did. She was someone he didn't want to end up alone with at any time this evening. She'd be too curious. No telling what she was liable to ask him.

She had to be in her late fifties yet looked more like Dallas and Dakota's sister. And like her two daughters, she was truly beautiful. She sure as hell didn't come off as a biology professor.

Tilly brought out their drinks and then took orders from the others for refills. No one demurred, which suited Eric fine. The more relaxed they all were, the better the evening was likely to go.

While Andrea instructed Tilly on dinner, he checked out the three Shea women. Any one of them easily could have enjoyed a lucrative modeling career. They had that look that brought ad campaigns to life. Horn had seen it in Dallas. That's why he wanted her.

He couldn't think about Horn right now. Or his demands. Later tonight would be soon enough. When they were alone, back at Eric's place. He'd lay the whole thing out for Dallas. The offer was good. She could make a lot of money, and with a three-year contract there'd be security, as well.

He glanced from Dallas to Dakota to Andrea and realized his confidence had slipped the minute he'd seen the three women together. They all looked like models, yet they'd chosen traditional careers rather than trading on their beauty. Maybe modeling was taboo. Too frivolous.

Of course, he still didn't know what Dallas did, which irked the hell out of him. All he knew is that she'd modeled once. Maybe she was trying to get into acting and was embarrassed to admit it. That would work in his favor. As Horn's spokesperson, she'd be seen all over the tristate area.

"So, Eric, tell us what you do," Andrea said, and Eric had to quickly regroup.

All eyes on him, he smiled. "Advertising. I work for Webber and Thornton."

"Oh." Andrea's lips lifted in approval. "Where?"

"Manhattan."

"What exactly do you do for them?"

"I'm an ad exec. I devise slogans, print ads, commercials, billboards—anything that sells the product."

"How nice. Sounds productive." She slanted Dallas a brief look that made her stiffen. "Have you two known each other long?"

"A few weeks," Dallas said quickly and then stared pointedly out at the pool. "Did you have it tiled again?"

Harrison sighed with a hint of disgust. "Your mother didn't like the dark-blue-and-green combination."

"But you just had it done last year."

Andrea sniffed and picked up her glass. Two lone ice cubes clinked together.

"Touchy subject." Cody gave Dallas a warning look. "Let's drop it." His hair was darker than the rest of the family's, and his eyes were closer to Dakota's color. Good-looking guy but too serious for the camera.

"Got it." Dallas picked up her wine and sipped.

Eric turned to Andrea, almost as if he'd sensed her stare.

She smiled. "What else should we know about you, Eric? Where are you from? Where did you meet our Dallas? Not at work, I'm sure."

"Mother."

"I'm just making conversation, dear." She met Dallas's gaze and held it. "Not to worry."

"Yes, after all, Clair already has gotten the third degree," Harrison said. "I think your mother should have been the one who went to law school."

Eric smiled. No one else did. Apparently Harrison wasn't just teasing, given the tense looks exchanged by his two daughters.

Tilly showed up with a tray, and as everyone busied themselves with claiming their respective drinks and sampling the crab-stuffed mushrooms, the tension quickly passed. Before she left, Tilly informed them that dinner would be served in half an hour.

"Excuse us for a moment, would you?" Dallas said as she rose from the table. "I'd like to show Eric Mother's garden before the sun sets completely."

Eric got up just as Andrea said, "Really, Dallas, we just met the man. Must you drag him away?"

"Good idea. Check out the roses," Dakota said quickly. "The salmon-colored ones are awesome."

"The garden lights will come on at any moment. You can go for a stroll later." Andrea waved a hand as if the matter were closed.

"We won't be long." Dallas took his hand. With her other one she grabbed her glass of wine. Even after their short acquaintance he recognized the stubborn set of her jaw and didn't argue.

He did give the others an apologetic shrug of his shoulders as he was led away. Not that he wouldn't rather be alone with Dallas, but he didn't want to piss off Andrea either. The woman obviously could be a real pain, but she was Dallas's mother and he preferred she be on his side.

Frankly he wasn't sorry Dallas had chosen that moment to liberate them. He hated the eventual turn Andrea's question would take. Hated admitting he was from Pittsburgh. That his family was a bunch of steelworkers. Hated even more that he felt that way.

As soon as they got past the white gazebo on the other side of the pool, Dallas mumbled under her breath, "God, why did I come here? I should have known better."

"Hey, come on. It's not so bad."

She looked at him with miserable blue eyes. "Plus, I drag you here to suffer, too."

"Fair is fair. I dragged you to Horn's party." He squeezed her hand. "Seriously everything's been fine. I feel totally comfortable."

"Right." She withdrew her hand and sipped her wine, staring out over a sea of yellow and pink roses sheltered by an ivy-covered brick wall separating their property from their neighbor's.

"Look, I don't understand your family dynamics. Obviously there's an undercurrent I don't get. But I am sorry you're annoyed." He decided not to tell her that he thought she was overreacting.

"No, I assure you, you don't get it. Hell, I don't totally get it." She bit her lower lip. "Sorry, I didn't mean to snap."

He remained silent for several moments, not sure what to say. He really didn't know this woman. Not the way he wanted to. All he could do was change the subject.

"This garden is something. It's been so damn hot the last couple of weeks, I'm surprised these roses held up."

She smiled as if she knew he had no idea what he was talking about. Maybe roses liked the heat. What the hell did he know about flowers or gardens? Not a Pittsburgh boy like him.

Dallas leaned against him, and they looked out over the mass of roses and ivy and some other little white flowers he didn't recognize—miniature roses maybe. Clinging to a vine, they climbed over the top layer of a white flagstone fountain nestled in the corner.

She breathed in the heady scent. "They are beautiful. Remind me to snitch a few before we leave. Look, those are the salmon-colored ones Dakota was talking about. I'm definitely swiping one of those."

He slid an arm around her shoulders. "Your mom doesn't seem like the type to garden. Of course, she doesn't seem like a biology teacher either."

"Don't let her hear you refer to her as a 'teacher.'"

"Excuse me. Professor."

Dallas laughed softly. "That woman hasn't seen the inside of a classroom in years. She's the head of research."

"Ah, that I can see."

"As far as gardening, the closest she comes is putting on a hat and sunglasses to come out and supervise their gardener."

He grinned. "Gotta admit, that would be my idea of gardening."

Her lips curved in a grudging smile. "Okay, I'll concede that one."

The lights came on, and Dallas jumped a little. He held her tighter, inhaling the vanilla scent from her hair. Man, what he wouldn't give to lay her down right here, in the middle of all those roses. Naked.

"What are you thinking?" she asked, looking up at him, a smile dancing at the corners of her mouth.

"Why?"

"You started breathing hard."

He laughed. "You don't want to know."

Her eyebrows went up, and she drew the tip of her finger across his lower lip. "Try me."

After glancing over his shoulder, he whispered, "What time do they go to bed?"

That startled a loud laugh out of her, and she quickly covered her mouth with her hand. "Not here. Not in this lifetime. I'd rather run naked around Columbus Circle."

"Hmm, that has possibilities."

She bumped him with her hip. "The lights make the garden look almost magical, don't they?"

"So, you're not going for it, huh?"

"You are crazy." She bumped him again, which wasn't helping to sidetrack him. "Now, can we please enjoy the moment? Eventually we do have to go back to the patio."

"We do?"

She turned to look at him.

"Only kidding."

"No, you're not. But that's okay." Something caught her attention and she squinted. "Looks like there's an opening in the wall."

"An opening?"

"Yeah, see where some of the bricks have crumbled. We could be out of here before they knew we were gone."

He laughed. "You wouldn't do that."

"Bet me."

"No, because then you'll do it." He turned her to face him. "You'd make me look bad to your parents."

"Why would you care?"

Eric brushed the side of her jaw, liking the silky feel of her skin. Remembering how soft her back was, the inside of her thighs, her perfect breasts. "I plan on sticking around for a while. That's why."

"A while, huh?"

"A long while."

"We'll see," she murmured just before he kissed her.

At least, that's what he thought he heard. But it made no sense. Unless she figured he wasn't a commitment kind of guy. The only way she could have arrived at that was by Tom.

He pulled back. The mood was ruined. "What do you mean by that?"

She slowly opened her eyes. "What?"

"You don't think we have something going on here."

"Of course I do."

"What did Tom tell you?"

She looked as if she were about to deny Tom's duplicity, but then she sighed and said, "Just enough for me to feel safe showing up at the party."

"Okay." He smiled. "That's progress. Now I know I'm not crazy."

She didn't return the smile but moved away and drained the rest of her wine. "We'd better go back. The sooner we eat dinner, the sooner we can leave."

He didn't like her attitude. Textbook passive-aggressive behavior. "Sorry if I ruined your fun."

She touched his arm, and when her lips lifted, it was in such a sad smile that he softened. "It was a mistake to bring you here. I'm sorry."

"Why was it a mistake?"

Her brows lifted in surprise, and then she gave a helpless shrug. "My mother— I have too many issues with her. I think each time I come home it will be different, but it never is."

"Turn around."

"Excuse me?"

He took her by the shoulders and prodded her into giving him her back. "You're tense," he said as he started massaging the tight muscles around her neck.

"No kidding."

Eric smiled. "We'll get you to relax."

"Good luck." She sighed and then moaned a little when he worked on a particularly tight knot. "She irritates me just being in the same vicinity. She could be somewhere in the house and I have no idea what she's doing and she still irritates me."

He chuckled and kept working. She was tight, all right. Tomorrow he'd treat her to a professional massage. The new Hush Hotel had a couples' massage that was supposed to be pretty awesome. He'd have to call and see if you needed to be a registered guest to use the service.

"It's not her fault. In fact, some of it's mine. I totally get that, in spite of all my childish carrying on." She laughed softly. "I'm her daughter and she wants what's best for me. The problem is, what she thinks is best, I don't."

"Gee, never heard that one before."

She hooked her arm around and pinched his waist.

"Hey, no manhandling the masseur."

"Like you'd be so lucky."

"Good point." He hesitated. She was starting to relax, and he didn't want to stir things up. But he'd have to know sooner or later if modeling was one of the issues that polarized them. Selfishly, later was out. Once back at his place, he didn't want to ruin the mood by bringing up Horn. "I have a question."

"Uh-huh."

"Does your mother object to your modeling?"

"No. But, of course, I really don't model anymore. But she's never had a problem with it as long as it's tasteful. Even Dakota did some modeling for a couple of local stores while she was in college."

Relief washed over him.

"Now, if either of us had decided we wanted to model and skip college, that would have been a major problem."

"Understandable. Only a few models make really good money. Unfortunately it isn't as glamorous as it looks, and their shelf life is shorter than a jar of peanut butter."

"Amen. That's why I quit."

Eric had to tamp down his excitement. None of those problems were attached to Horn's contract.

She sighed and covered one of his hands with hers. "As wonderful as this has been, I think it's time to go back."

"To Manhattan?" he joked.

"I wish. To the lion's den."

15

TILLY ANNOUNCED THAT DINNER was going to be ready in ten minutes. Dallas knew her mother wouldn't be content to stay out of the final preparations, and when, true to form, she headed for the kitchen, Dallas followed.

She'd actually thought tonight might work out. She'd psyched herself up for two days, telling herself it would be okay to bring Eric. The conversation would remain neutral because she'd received her mother's reassurance that she'd make nice.

Clair's presence changed everything. Damn it. It blew all illusion of control.

"Why didn't you tell me Cody was bringing someone?" she asked as soon as they were in private. Tilly was there, of course, standing at the butcher-block island, tossing some field greens in a glass bowl, but Dallas trusted her implicitly.

"I'm not sure I knew when you called." After setting her wineglass on the granite counter, Andrea picked up a fork Tilly had left beside the stove and stuck it in the rib roast. She made a face. "Tilly, are you sure this is done enough? It looks awfully rare."

Tilly grabbed the fork from her and waved her away.

"Go back to your guests and let me handle dinner. The meat is still cooking while it rests. In ten minutes it'll be just the way you like it." Tilly winked at Dallas.

They must have had this conversation twenty times in as many years. But Andrea always had to stick her nose in things.

"Dallas, bring out your grandmother's silver tureen," her mother said. "I think we'll serve the consommé from the table instead of bringing it to the dining room in individual bowls."

"No, we're not. I have everything set out already." Tilly looked at Dallas. "Would you please get your mother out of here?"

"Really, Tilly, I'm only trying to help." Andrea grabbed her drink off the counter and turned to leave in a huff. Amazing how Tilly was the only one who could get away with speaking to her like that. Dallas never could figure it out. Not even her father dared being that high-handed—not overtly, anyway.

"Wait, Mother."

She stopped and looked impatiently at Dallas.

"I want tonight to go smoothly, okay?" Dallas said slowly, enunciating every word.

"Don't be absurd."

"Please, Mother, keep your promise that you won't manipulate the conversation as a means of attacking my job. Am I clear?"

"Everything isn't about you. You're old enough to know that."

Dallas shook her head. "I wish *you* understood that.

Why you have to keep—" Dallas stopped herself. This wasn't going anywhere. It never did. "Never mind."

Her mother blinked, and something changed in her expression. Regret flickered in her eyes. "I know you think I ride you too hard, that I meddle too much. But you're so damn smart, Dallas, what kind of mother would I be if I let you slide in life?"

"You're right. I think you push too hard."

"I probably do. Your father and I have always been proud of all three of you kids. But you were always the brightest, the one with the most potential."

Dallas stared in disbelief. For years she'd felt like the runt of the litter. The one who'd always disappointed them.

"Someday when you're a mother maybe you'll understand." She touched Dallas's arm in an uncharacteristic gesture of concern, and Dallas's defenses began to crumble. "I'm glad to see you brought a decent man with you."

Just like that, the forgiving mood was shot to hell. "A man who gets his hands dirty making a living can be just as decent."

Andrea huffed. "You know what I mean. Must you take everything wrong?"

"As long as you keep giving me ammunition." Dallas exhaled and sheepishly met her mother's eyes. "I'm sorry. I really am. I don't want to argue."

Andrea looked at her a long, silent moment and then sighed. "Well, as you've often pointed out, what you do for a living is your business. I am curious, though, what does Eric think about it?"

Dallas hesitated. The question had taken her aback. She swallowed, tried to come up with a flip remark and couldn't.

Her mother stared with open curiosity, and then a slow, amused smile lifted the corners of her mouth. "He doesn't know, does he?"

Dallas stiffened. God, all she wanted to do was leave. Right now. Get back to Manhattan. To Eric's apartment, where anything seemed possible.

The pity that entered her mother's eyes was almost more than Dallas could take. "If you're too embarrassed to tell him," she said gently, "then, honey, you've got a lot to think about."

DURING DINNER THE CONVERSATION centered mostly on a volatile court case that was in the news but to which none of the Shea legal eagles had any affiliation. Lots of opinions, though. Which made for a lively discussion.

These were the times that Dallas missed. When she was in high school and her friends would come over for dinner, they were always surprised. The expectation was that dinner at the Sheas' would be a quiet, dignified affair. Rarely was that the case.

Since Dallas had little opinion on the subject and wasn't about to get into another debate with Cody over justification of the death penalty, she got up to help Tilly with dessert. Deeply involved in the conversation, Eric glanced at her and smiled before returning another of Cody's volleys. He looked as if he were actually enjoying himself, and even her brother seemed more animated and taking great pleasure in the challenging arguments Eric presented.

This time she didn't have to ask Dakota to babysit Eric in her absence. Not just because the conversational tide was unlikely to change but because she knew her mother would derail any personal talk of Dallas.

Odd, really, that she'd consider her mother an ally. But she'd been more subdued during the meal, sitting quietly and thoughtfully, sometimes glancing at Dallas and giving her an encouraging smile. Weird. Totally weird. But there it was.

She carried two stacks of dirty dinner dishes into the kitchen with her and placed them in the sink. Tilly was making coffee and she turned around when she heard Dallas.

"Leave those," she said. "I'll load the dishwasher while you eat dessert."

"I have a better idea." Dallas turned on the water to rinse the plates. "Eat dessert with us."

"I'm watching my sugar."

"Then have fruit. You're part of the family. You should be eating with us." Dallas looked around, suddenly interested in what Tilly had made, and spotted the apple-caramel pie. Oh, God. Not good. Dallas's favorite. She could eat the whole thing.

"You sound like your mother. Like I've told her many times, I eat my big meal in the middle of the day."

"I sound like my mother?" Dallas said, aware it sounded like an insult when Tilly slid her a disapproving frown.

Snorting, Tilly wiped her hands on her apron and then opened the refrigerator and brought out a stainless-steel bowl of freshly whipped cream. "Yes, your mother. She always insists I eat with her and your father. And one of these days you're going to realize how much you two are alike. No wonder you're always butting heads like two bighorn sheep. I've never encountered two more stubborn women."

"That's not true. Not about me, anyway."

Tilly gave her an amused look.

"Just because I want to live my own life doesn't make me stubborn." Dallas stuck her finger in the bowl of whipped cream and got her hand slapped.

"There's living your own life and then there's rubbing it in everyone's face."

Dallas gasped. "I've never done that."

"No?"

"Of course not."

The older woman smiled.

"Tilly, come on, you're making me feel awful."

"If it's not true, there's nothing to feel awful about." She put an arm around Dallas's waist and hugged her. "I love you. You three kids are like my own. I don't like to see any of you hurting."

"I know, Tilly. I love you, too." Dallas swallowed back the lump forming in her throat. She didn't know what else to say. Tilly had always been fair and a straight talker. She wouldn't purposely needle Dallas. The thought that she'd disappointed the woman made Dallas ill.

"All right." She returned to the freshly brewed coffee and got out a silver carafe. "Get your fanny back into the dining room and take the dessert plates and the pie with you. I don't trust you with the whipped cream. I'll take that out myself, along with the coffee."

Glad to be back on playful ground, Dallas sniffed. "You don't trust me?"

"With my life? Yes. With whipped cream? No." Tilly lightly smacked her on her backside. "Now get."

"All right already," she said and grabbed the stack of plates.

"Use a pot holder. The pie is still warm."

Tilly's caramel-apple pie was to die for. But warm? Dallas sighed in anticipation. "Did I tell you how much I love you?"

Tilly chuckled and winked. "My dear girl, I would bake you a pie anytime you wanted."

"I know." Dallas had to shut up before she got all teary-eyed. It wasn't even that time of the month. Why the hell was she feeling so emotional all of a sudden?

She took a deep breath and then got out a tray, not trusting herself to carry both the pie and plates out to the dining room safely. After she'd carefully balanced her load, she picked up the tray and backed her way through the swinging door.

She used her hip to keep the door open until she made it to the dining room on the other side. Just as she let go, her foot caught on the edge of the door. She stumbled forward and watched in horror as the pie flew off the tray and splattered across the hardwood floor.

ADHERING TO HER WISHES, THE goodbyes were said inside. No more sympathetic looks, no more idiotic jokes, no annoying fanfare as they left the porch. Thank God.

Dallas slid into the backseat of the car Eric had hired, and he climbed in beside her. She'd huddled closer to the opposite door, but he put an arm around her and drew her against him, to which she responded with mixed feelings. Part of her wanted to be left alone to wallow in self-pity, but the other part needed his soothing touch, needed the reassurance that he still wanted her.

It wasn't just about her clumsiness that had her fraying at the seams. Accidents happened. Of course, she wished she hadn't totally ruined dessert, but hey… What bothered her more were the crazy thoughts running through her head. Ideas spawned by her mother and Tilly.

The car left her parents' circular drive and sped off toward Manhattan. Traffic in and around the city was brutal at any given time, but Saturday night had to be the worst. Inbound was horrible. Nearly ten already, and people were just headed in. It felt as if she'd never get home.

Eric kissed her hair. "Hey, are you still sulking?"

"I'm not sulking."

"Wrong word. Stewing."

"Yes, I'm still stewing."

He laughed, hugged her closer. "I knew you were anxious to leave, but that was a bit extreme."

"Are you trying to make me feel better? It's definitely not working."

Sighing, he rested his head on top of hers. "I liked your family."

"That scares me."

"Come on, seriously."

"I am serious."

He straightened to look at her. "What problem could you possibly have with Dakota? It's obvious she adores her older sister."

Dallas leaned back and smiled. She knew that. "We get along great. Of course, we're the most alike."

"And Cody was a little dull at first, but he was great once he warmed up. He isn't all that conservative when it comes to legal issues. He believes in something and he's passionate about it. I admire that."

"I have to admit I did enjoy him tonight. I just wish Clair had a little more personality. He needs someone to give him a jolt once in a while."

"Yeah, I can see that." He started to laugh and then pretended to clear his throat.

She looked at him. "What?"

"Nothing."

She elbowed him in the ribs, and he grunted. "Don't give me that. What were you thinking?"

"About your father. If I were ever hauled into court, I'd want someone like him hearing my case. He seems reasonable and fair. I like him. Part of the dying breed who still watches baseball. Does my heart good."

"Uh-huh." She gave him a "nice try" look.

"And then there's Tilly. What's not to like about her? She's a doll."

She loved that he'd included Tilly as part of the family. "You still haven't told me why you were laughing. Although I have a good guess."

"You first."

"Chicken."

"But I have my good qualities."

She grinned. "It's about my mother."

"Sort of. I was thinking how she probably gives your dad all the attitude he needs."

"And then some."

"But I liked her," he added quickly.

"Right."

"I did. At first, I admit, she gave me the willies. No offense," he said with a wry smile. "But then later she mellowed. The way she brushed off your dropping the pie and then joking about not needing the calories, well, I thought that was nice."

"Yeah." Dallas had been a little surprised at her laid-back reaction. Maybe she'd figured she'd beaten up on Dallas enough for one evening.

The unfair thought left Dallas uncomfortable. Her mother had given her a lot to think about. Dallas couldn't blame her for that. Nor could she blame her mother for being right. Damn it. The idea chafed.

"Are you stewing again?"

"Now I'm sulking."

"Not allowed." He lifted her chin and brought her around to face him, then brushed her lips with his. "This is a no-sulking zone."

"I could wait until we get home."

He frowned, thinking a moment, and then shook his head. "Better get it out of your system. I have plans."

"Oh? Such as?"

He slid a hand between her thighs.

She jumped. "Oh."

"Need I demonstrate further?" He lowered his voice, prompting the driver to glance in the rearview mirror.

Dallas met his eyes and quickly dropped her gaze. She wagged a scolding finger at Eric, which he grabbed and sucked into his mouth. She got the giggles and couldn't stop until she had to gulp for air.

"Damn." Eric shot a sidelong glance at the driver. "He thinks we're having much more fun than we are."

That started Dallas giggling all over again. Not because that idea was particularly funny but because she needed the release. Needed to laugh or she might start crying.

Tilly's gentle criticism had gotten to her the worst. Tilly had never lied to Dallas. Ever. Tilly had always been supportive, always fair and always available with a shoulder for Dallas to lean on or cry on. In fact, she was that way with everyone in the family. And she thought Dallas had rubbed her rebellion in her parents' face.

Had she? Certainly when she was younger, just out of college, she'd done her share of flaunting her independence. She'd ended up paying for her own graduate studies as a result. Anyway, she'd backed off since then. The construction job didn't count. That had nothing to do with rebellion. It was good, honest work, and she needed the money.

Her conscience whispered otherwise, and she shifted positions as if the maneuver would ease her emotional discomfort.

Eric obviously misunderstood and pulled her closer. She smelled the cognac lingering on his breath, the musky masculine scent that was all his. "Okay if we go back to my place?" he whispered into her hair and then rubbed his clean-shaven chin there.

She hesitated, unsure what kind of company she'd make. And then he tilted her chin up and kissed her, and she knew she'd be a lot more miserable at home, fretting over what she was missing.

16

ERIC HAD A PROBLEM. HE closed his apartment door behind him and watched Dallas sink into the couch and kick off her shoes. She was in a strange mood. Even before she'd splattered the pie on the hardwood dining room floor. The memory brought an involuntary grin to his face, which he promptly stifled.

The thing was, he needed to give Horn an answer on Monday, but Eric didn't think now was the right time. Maybe later, after she'd relaxed. After they'd made love.

Maybe he could even talk her into spending the night. Then over breakfast he'd lay it all out. God, he couldn't even recall the last time he'd let a woman spend the night.

He tossed his keys on the kitchen counter. "How about something to drink?"

She groaned. "I think I've probably had enough."

"You only had two glasses, but I have orange juice, or I can make coffee."

Dallas shook her head and smiled. "I'm good."

"Yes, you are," he said with a suggestive grin, moving in beside her and sliding an arm around her. "Very good, in fact."

She didn't hesitate to snuggle up to him and lay her cheek against his chest. "Tell me something."

He picked up a lock of her honey-colored hair and let the silken strands fall between his fingers. "Anything."

"Tell me about your family."

"Like what?"

"I know you have two brothers and you're the middle one. But that's all."

The subject was bound to come up. He still didn't like it. But he wouldn't lie. Not that he would volunteer more than her curiosity demanded, either. "Well, I think I told you I grew up in Pittsburgh. All of my family is still there. My parents still live in the same house where I grew up."

"Sounds like my family."

"Nope, my family is nothing like yours."

She flinched and moved away, and he knew she'd taken it wrong.

"My family is strictly blue-collar," he quickly clarified. "Our dinner conversation tended to center around who the Steelers were going to cream that weekend."

"That's football, right?"

"See what I mean? That question alone would be considered sacrilege where I come from."

She grinned. "What happens when the Steelers lose?"

"Two days of lamenting what a bum the quarterback is and how the coach has no business coaching in the pros. And then they start getting pumped for the next weekend's game."

"They? You didn't participate?"

Smiling, he ran a hand down her thigh. "You caught me."

She shifted closer again. "Then you went to college?"

"Only one in the family."

"Go back to visit often?"

"Mostly just on holidays. I've got a bunch of nieces and nephews I like to see. And of course, my parents."

"And your bothers?"

"Sometimes there's tension. They think I'm uppity."

"Are you?"

"What do you think?"

She stared down at his fly and gave her head a sorrowful shake. "You're not uppity."

He barked out a laugh.

"But I can take care of that," she said, sliding her hand across his thigh.

That's all it took, and he started getting pretty damn uppity. She undid his belt buckle, and he relaxed his head back against the cushions, his arms stretched out along the back of the couch, and he watched her.

She took her time, unzipping an inch, kissing him through the fabric, unzipping some more. She was making him crazy, just as he was sure she intended. When he lifted his ass so she could pull down his waistband, she ignored him and pushed the front of his slacks aside. She found the opening in his boxers and freed his cock. He sprung up hard and ready.

She touched her tongue to the tip, and he shuddered. She glanced up, took another lick and smiled. "Did you say something?"

"Help."

She laughed. "Don't you worry. A little CPR should take care of the problem." She lowered her head, but fool that he was, he stopped her, and she blinked up in surprise.

"Stay the night."

A small frown drew her brows together. "I don't know."

"We'll get up early, have breakfast and then you can do whatever."

A slow smile curved her lips just as she ran her tongue around the head. "You stopped me for that?"

He groaned and closed his eyes. How could he think straight when she was doing that?

She took him into her mouth, and he forgot about anything besides her warm breath and talented tongue. She went from gentle swirls to assault mode and back again, keeping him off balance, taking him to the brink and then reeling him back in.

Until he couldn't take it anymore. He tried to get up, intent on reciprocating, but she gave it all she had, and the explosion started before he had another coherent thought.

DALLAS AWOKE AROUND DAWN. Bits of dusky light seeped through the blinds. She tried to roll over to see the alarm clock, but Eric had curled around her, his chest pressed to her back, the stubble from his chin tickling her shoulder. Not even her moving around woke him. He snuggled closer, his semihard penis nudging her backside.

Smiling, she thought about waking him. She'd give him two minutes tops to get hard enough to get inside her. The boy certainly had stamina. Last night alone had proved that fact. They'd made love twice before they'd even gotten to bed and then once more sometime between one and three. She'd nodded off after that.

On the nightstand was her watch, and she slowly reached for it. She yawned and blinked at the blurry face until it cleared. Nine-thirty! It couldn't be that late. She blinked a couple more times. Still nine-thirty. That gave her less than two hours to shower, dress and make it home before Nancy and Yvette got there.

Slowly she pushed back the covers and inched away from Eric. His arm came around her waist and he pulled her back against him.

"Morning," he murmured into her hair and then planted a kiss on the back of her neck.

"Go back to sleep," she whispered, knowing that wouldn't happen. Knowing she wasn't going to make it out of bed anytime soon. And not really caring.

"Right." He kissed her again, her neck, each shoulder, then started down her spine.

"Eric, I have to go."

"What time is it?"

"Nine-thirty."

"No kidding." He cupped her breast and teased the already tightened nipple.

She closed her eyes. "Eric..."

"Hmm."

"You promised."

He lightly bit the side of her neck and then rolled onto his back and sighed. "I was a fool, but you're right. I did."

Dallas turned over and laid a hand on his chest. His hair was sticking up on one side and his chin was dark with stubble. He looked adorable. "Of course, I could spare about twenty minutes."

A roguish smile started at the corners of his mouth, but then he frowned, pushed a frustrated hand through his hair and said, "Tell you what, I'll go make coffee while you take a shower."

"Sure." She shrugged a shoulder and turned to get up, but her disappointment must have shown because he caught her arm and pulled her close again.

"I'd like nothing better than to stay in bed with you all day, but you have things to do, and I have something I'd like to discuss with you before you leave."

She didn't like the serious sound of that. "Like what?"

"Nothing bad. Relax."

"Well, let's talk now."

"You sure you don't want to be ready to go."

"Why? Am I going to want to run screaming from the apartment?"

He grinned. "You have quite an imagination."

"It's getting worse by the second."

"Okay." He sat up, letting the sheet bunch at his waist, and she kept her attention on his face, not wanting to be distracted by his yummy chest. Apparently he didn't have the same compunction. His gaze went directly to her breasts. He noisily cleared his throat. "On second thought, I think we'd better get dressed."

She grunted in exasperation, her curiosity about to burst. "I want to know now or I will hurt you."

He smiled. "Sounds promising."

"Damn it, Eric."

"Remember Lawrence Horn?"

"Of course."

"He came to my office on Thursday. He wants you to be his spokesperson."

"His what?"

"That's broad, I know. Basically he wants your face to be associated with his company and he wants me to design ads based on that."

Dumbfounded, she fell back against the pillows.

"The money would be good. I'm thinking six figures over the life of, say, a three-year contract."

She exhaled slowly, her thoughts one big jumble. This was her chance to get out of the construction business. And she wouldn't have to eat crow, either. Not when the job had landed in her lap. But did she want to get back in that crazy business? She was older now and a little out of shape, less tolerant of sadistic photographers who liked to harp on every little flaw.

God, she'd be like Wendy—desperate, chasing after the next gig, pathetically ignoring the fading of youth. She took a deep calming breath and looked at Eric. "I don't think—"

He put a refraining finger to her lips. "I know what you're going to say. But this is different. No cattle calls. No worrying about paying the rent on time. Best of all, no competition. This is a sure thing."

Of course, he knew what she was thinking. They'd had a similar conversation before about why she didn't like modeling. But he didn't know the rest. She already had a job. And it was a far cry from smiling pretty for the camera.

"Look, you'd call the shots on this. We'd work around your schedule. There'd be print ads, commercials, billboards—the usual. I haven't done anything on it yet. Not until I talked to you." He gave her a wry smile. "You realize you still haven't told me what you do."

"No?"

He gave her a long-suffering look, and then his gaze narrowed. "You're a lawyer, too, aren't you?"

"God, no." She hesitated. "Three in the family are enough." Now would be the perfect time to tell him. On the other hand, if she accepted the offer, why bother? He wouldn't need to know. What she did for a living now would be irrelevant.

Her mother's words came back to her and she tensed. Not that Dallas was embarrassed. It wasn't as if she were a stripper or made porn movies, for God's sake.

Eric touched her arm, bringing her out of her preoccupation. "What are you thinking?"

"Frankly, about how much I have to do today. And now this." She waved a frustrated hand. "Well, I've got a lot of thinking to do."

"Right." He squeezed her arm. "Maybe we could meet for dinner? I'm sure you'll have questions."

"I have one now. How will my decision affect you?"

He leaned his head back and glanced at the ceiling,

one side of his mouth lifting slowly. "Horn's an important client and he wants you."

"And your boss has told you to make it happen."

"Of course he wants to keep Horn happy. But this has nothing to do with us. Whatever decision you make has to be what's best for you."

She took a deep breath. Her decision would have more to do with their relationship than he thought. The image he created in Horn's ad campaign would be exactly the kind of woman Eric wanted. At the thought, her defenses started to rise. Stupid, since she couldn't blame him for something he didn't even know was happening.

Besides, she was hardly being fair, having withheld information about herself. Hadn't she also created a certain image? A very wrong image. The idea stung.

"I'll have to let you know later about dinner," she said and started to get up.

"Wait." He tugged on her arm, coaxing her back beside him. He drew the back of his hand down her cheek. "No matter what, we won't let whatever happens affect us, okay?"

She nodded. "Deal."

Their lips met, and she wanted to crawl back under the covers and pretend he was right. That everything would be okay. Only somehow deep down she knew better.

WHEN DALLAS ANSWERED THE DOOR, she was surprised to find not just Nancy and Yvette but also Jan and Sally standing in the corridor.

"Hope you don't mind us tagging along," Jan said, leading the others into the apartment and then heading for the kitchen with a grocery sack in each hand. She planted both bags on the counter, which pretty much eliminated room for anything else.

"I'll grab a beanbag chair from my room." Dallas hesitated, tamping down her annoyance as she watched Jan take out six-packs of beer and diet cola and a box of cheese crackers.

This wasn't supposed to be a party. They'd said they wanted to talk to her. Fine. But she had other things to do this afternoon. Like mope around the apartment in indecision. Talk to Wendy and Trudie. Let them tell her what an idiot she was for not immediately signing on the dotted line before Horn changed his mind.

Her head hadn't stopped spinning since Eric had told her about Horn's offer. Why she had the slightest hesitation, she couldn't explain. She didn't even get why the idea made her so edgy. A contract would lock her in and give her income and insurance while she figured out what she wanted to do when she grew up. Most people would consider the decision a no-brainer. A normal person would have jumped at the chance.

She brought back the leather beanbag chair—a holdover from her college-dorm days—and placed it under the small window that offered an excellent view of the dirty brick building several yards away.

"You wanna beer or a soda?" Jan asked as she handed a cola to Yvette. Nancy and Sally already had beers in their hands.

"Uh, neither, thanks." Dallas sat on the floor near the beanbag chair. "What's going on?"

Jan grabbed a cola and they all sat down. When the other three looked to Jan, she snorted and said, "We came up with something that the other women might go for."

Dallas let out a slow breath. This was good. Very good. They'd come up with an idea on their own. They were looking to Jan for leadership and not Dallas. This was excellent, in fact. "What's that?"

"We're gonna do the petition thing. Kind of. We're thinkin' maybe more like a letter." Jan shrugged, glanced at the others. "You know, real detailed, like, about the shit that's been going on."

"But no names mentioned," Yvette added, her hands gripping the cola can as if it were life support. "Right?"

Nancy patted her leg. "Right. We just state the stuff we want to see change."

"Or that we won't put up with anymore," Jan said, and everyone nodded.

"Okay. Good." Dallas smiled. This was nothing new, it's what they'd been talking about all along. She didn't bother pointing that out. No need. They'd finally accepted what had to be done. That's all that was important. "Have you talked to the others?"

"Yeah." Jan glanced at Nancy. "They like the idea."

Sally snorted. "I wouldn't say 'like.'"

"Okay, but they'll hang with us." Jan sipped her cola, her gaze on Dallas. "As long as you write the letter."

"No problem. I'll get to work on it right away."

Yvette's sigh was pure relief, and then she smiled. "I might even have a beer."

Nancy elbowed Jan. Subtly, but Dallas caught it.

"Anything else?" she asked, even though she could see trouble in Jan's and Nancy's eyes.

"Yeah." Jan shrugged. "No big deal, though."

Nancy glared at Jan when she hesitated, then turned to Dallas. "We want you to sign the letter."

"By myself?"

Jan wiped her mouth with the back of her hand. "Not exactly. We'll all sign our names on the next page, like we're supporting you."

Dallas laughed. "What am I? The sacrificial lamb?"

They all stared at her, clearly confused, and then Jan said, "They're gonna know you wrote it." She snorted and glanced at the others. "None of us would know how to write that kind of letter."

Dallas sighed. "That isn't the point."

"You wouldn't get in trouble, right?" Yvette leaned forward, her elbows resting on her thighs, her hands clasped tightly around the can. "You said it would be illegal to fire us."

"Absolutely." Dallas thought a moment. "I could get my sister to write the letter. Some of you met Dakota at our last meeting."

Nancy's eyes widened. "The lawyer?"

Dallas nodded, already knowing it was a bad idea. Too formal. Too threatening.

"That would piss off the suits. Big-time." Jan got up

and grabbed the box of cheese crackers. "You're one of us, Dallas. Better it comes from you."

"Better it comes from all of us," Dallas corrected.

"True." Jan passed the crackers around. No one seemed interested. "But I don't think it's gonna fly any other way."

After a long stretch of silence, Nancy said, "This sucks, you guys. We're asking a lot from Dallas. It's not fair to lay this on her."

Sheepish looks were exchanged, and everyone nodded.

"Let's forget it." Yvette stood and squared her slim shoulders. With her brown hair pulled back in a pony-tail, she barely looked seventeen. "We can deal."

"Wait a minute." Dallas motioned for her to sit back down. "I didn't say I wouldn't do it."

Their expectant gazes riveted to her.

She took a deep breath, trying to stay calm, trying to stop the crazy thoughts from taking over. Ironic, really, that she was suddenly in such demand. Pulled from opposite ends of the spectrum. But only one side truly needed her.

"I'm saying that I'll think about it." Ludicrous to backpedal when she knew exactly what she had to do. *"I'll do it."*

17

"To tell you the truth, I don't know what the big deal is. I'd kill for something like this to fall in my lap. I'm jealous as hell." Wendy fished the green olive out of her martini and popped it into her mouth. She looked at Dallas over the rim of her glass. "You'd be silly to pass up an opportunity like this."

Trudie snorted and set down her Fuzzy Navel to glare at Wendy. "Of course it's a big deal. Dallas can't just desert her friends now."

"Did I suggest she desert them?" Wendy looked from Trudie to Dallas. "Anybody hear me say that? I'm just saying there's gotta be a way to work this out so she doesn't lose the contract."

Duh. Is that all? Dallas sighed and briefly closed her eyes. Thank God the neighborhood restaurant wasn't crowded. Only three other booths were occupied. If she screamed, there wouldn't be too many witnesses to her meltdown.

Her friends meant well, but they weren't helping. Besides, she was tired and cranky and feeling guilty for lying to Eric about why she couldn't see him tonight. She'd told him she had a work emergency, which wasn't a total lie. But what she should have done was gone ahead and met with him, explained her dilemma and let the chips fall where they may.

Of course, then he'd probably withdraw the offer, tell her she didn't have the right image after all. Not for Horn. Not for Eric. They didn't want just a pretty face. They wanted a total package, at least Eric did. And then if that was the case, screw him.

"Dallas?" Wendy waved a hand in front of her face. "What's going on in there?"

She shook her head. "I have never been so confused in my entire life."

"Okay, look. I think I'm missing something here." Wendy shot Trudie a warning glance. "You let me finish before you jump down my throat. This is how I see it. First, you do want the modeling job, right?"

Dallas nodded.

"But you feel an obligation to finish what you started with your buddies on the work crew, which I totally get. But why can't you do both? I mean, wouldn't it be kind of dramatic if you suddenly quit and, hell, lie, tell them you're quitting because of the harassment. That would work in everyone's favor."

"You don't understand. These guys have no conscience, plus they're sneaky and relentless. Those women would have no defense once I left."

Wendy sighed. "Well, Florence Nightingale, maybe your little chicks should just grow up."

"See? That's what I hate." Trudie glared at Wendy. "Do you have to be so snide? This is serious."

Just when Dallas figured the fireworks would start, Wendy gave them a wry smile and said, "I'm just saying—okay, really badly—but I want Dallas to think about herself for a change. She's bailed both of us out many times," she said, glancing at Trudie and then back to Dallas. "You're always there for everyone else. Do this for yourself."

"It's not that simple," Dallas murmured, sorry she'd involved them. They didn't understand, and she wasn't sure she wanted to let them in on her stupidity. The fantasy had taken over. She'd been Cinderella for several nights. And then it stretched out to a week, and now this.

"It can be."

"I agree with Wendy." Trudie sat back to nurse her Fuzzy Navel. "Eric said he'd work around your schedule. Maybe you're making a bigger deal out of this than it needs to be."

"Maybe." Dallas exhaled sharply. "Let's talk about something else."

"You don't look happy." Trudie sat forward again, concern darkening her heavily made-up eyes. "Was he freaked when you told him what you really do?"

Avoiding their eyes, Dallas grabbed her club soda, and it sloshed onto the table.

"Dallas?" They both said at the same time.

"What?"

"You haven't told him," Trudie said in utter amazement.

Wendy muttered a curse. "Dallas, you're probably more worried about your image than he is."

Dallas clenched her teeth at the stinging words. "Tomorrow night, okay. I'm telling him tomorrow night."

DALLAS HAD JUST CLOCKED OUT for the day when her cell phone rang. It was probably Eric again. He'd already called twice today. She hadn't picked up either time. Not that she was too chicken to talk to him. Well, there was that, too. But each time she'd been working, and the boss was strict about personal calls on company time.

She grabbed her lunch pail and the cell phone off her belt at the same time, hoping to get away from the machinery noise. The project was behind schedule, and half the guys were working overtime. She hadn't been asked if she wanted more hours, of course, nor had Nancy. After all, they weren't heads of households with wives and children to feed. Their attitude made her sick. Made her fighting mad. That's why she couldn't accept Eric's offer.

By the fourth ring she'd freed the phone from her belt and glanced at the caller ID. With a mixture of disappointment and relief she saw that it was Trudie and answered it.

"Dallas, thank God."

"What's wrong?"

"Where are you?"

"I just got off work. Trudie, you're scaring me. What's going on?"

"How fast can you get to the store?"

"Trudie!"

"You've got to do this for me. Starla is sick again, and

if I don't have someone in that window in one hour, I'm going to be in serious trouble."

Dallas put a hand to her throat and released a breath. "Damn it. You scared the hell out of me."

"Please, Dallas. I'll owe you big-time."

"You already do," she muttered, thinking about how this whole mess with Eric started. "I just got off work. I've got to shower and wash my hair and—"

"No, come straight here. We'll work all that out, even if we have to use the fitness center next door."

"You know I have to talk to Eric tonight."

"That's tonight?"

Dallas sighed and checked her watch. "Would I have to stay until nine?"

"Would eight work?"

"I'll be right there."

"I love you, kiddo." Trudie paused. "From what you said, Eric sounds like a great guy. Don't underestimate him."

"I know." She started to tell Trudie about her decision but stopped herself. No more discussion was needed. She knew what she had to do. "I've gotta go catch a cab if you want me there soon."

"Go."

They hung up, and Dallas hurried to the corner to catch a Yellow cab that had just dropped someone off. Once she climbed inside, she called Eric's number and got his voice mail. She left a message suggesting they meet later, close to nine, and tried not to dwell on how torturous it was going to be, stuck in that window, thinking about how she had to spill everything to Eric.

She reminded herself that she'd done nothing wrong. She'd never lied about herself. And she wasn't embarrassed, as her mother had hinted. Not really. Her work simply wasn't anything you discussed over dinner. It was boring, really.

Traffic wasn't horrendous yet, at least not by Manhattan standards, and she got to the corner of Lexington and Fifty-seventh in good time. There the bottleneck started, so she got out to walk the rest of the way. Everyone else was dressed in business attire, and she got several second looks and a few blatant stares that really irked her.

Damn, but she should have at least found a mirror. Made a few repairs. She always went straight home after work and changed out of her overalls, even if she was meeting Tony and some of the other guys for a beer. But here she was, in midtown no less, her hard hat in one hand and her lunch pail in the other. God only knew what her hair and face looked like. Trudie would pay dearly for this.

Dallas spotted her standing outside the store, waiting, with a bag in her hand. She was looking the other way, so Dallas couldn't get her attention. Especially not with all the pedestrians who seemed to have come out of nowhere, as if the recess bell had just rung. Good in a way, because people paid less attention to Dallas.

She narrowly dodged a man too busy talking on a cell phone to see her but then bumped into someone else.

"Excuse me," she said and looked up in into Eric's stunned eyes. Horrified, she tried to sidestep him. Disappear before his shock wore off. She ended up running into Tom. Literally.

He took her arm to keep her from stumbling, his face a mask of astonished disbelief.

"Dallas?"

She looked back to Eric. "Hi."

He stared at her for one very long, miserable moment. Then his gaze went to the Aladdin lunch pail, to the yellow hard hat, then returned to her face. "What are you doing?"

"I'm late," she said, backing away and bumping into a man who cursed when she smashed his white deli sack. "Sorry," she muttered to him. Then she said to Eric, "I really have to go. I'll talk to you later."

Eric watched her hurry through the crowd and meet up with a short, well-dressed woman who grabbed her arm and hustled her off in the other direction. Half of him wanted to follow them and the other half was too stunned to move.

"What the hell was that about?" Tom stood beside him, the two of them staring after her.

"I have no idea."

"We'd better move before we get trampled."

Eric seemed rooted to the spot. He couldn't get the image of her in dusty overalls and steel-toed boots out of his mind. Not just that. Her smudged face. Her hair a total mess, so dusty, it looked brown. He almost hadn't recognized her.

"Come on, Eric, or I'm going to Pete's without you."

"Yeah, okay," he said, taking a final look, even though she'd already disappeared. He finally turned around. A double shot of scotch sounded damn good about now.

HER HANDS SHAKING, DALLAS reached for the door handle. She'd already seen him through the window, sitting at the bar, staring at the baseball game on the wall-mounted television. The place was dim, not crowded, and for both those reasons she'd asked him to meet her here.

Not that she had to worry anymore about how she looked. She'd been cleaned up, coiffed and made up, thanks to one of the store's stylists. She looked just like the old Dallas. At least, the one Eric was used to.

If only she had told him before he'd seen her, she wouldn't be so nervous. Wouldn't feel guilty, as if she'd done something wrong, which she absolutely hadn't. She just wished her damn hands would stop trembling.

She opened the door and he looked over at her. He smiled, but it wasn't the same excited smile he normally gave her. He looked confused, maybe even apprehensive, and she didn't blame him. Nor did she blame him for the way he sized her up. Head to toe. As if trying to convince himself seeing her earlier had been a bad dream.

Clearing her throat, she took the stool next to him and smiled. "Hey."

"Hey back." He signaled the bartender. "Wine?" he asked her a little too politely, his tone a little distant.

Or was it her imagination? Was she seeing and hear-

ing what she expected to see and hear? "A triple martini would be much better."

He smiled.

She looked at the bartender. "Club soda, please."

"I'll have another," Eric told the man and then turned
back toward her but said nothing.

The silence got too maddening, and she pretended interest in the television. "So, who's winning?"

"I have no idea."

"Oh. I thought you were watching."

His gaze stayed on her. "Were you avoiding me
today?"

"No." She gave an emphatic shake of her head. "No,
really, I was working and couldn't pick up."

"Working?"

"Uh-huh," she said and pounced on the club soda the
bartender set in front of her. She hurriedly took a big
gulp. Too big. It made her cough.

"You okay?" He touched her arm, and the familiarity was so reassuring, she wanted to melt into him.

"Fine. Now. I was in the window again tonight. For
three hours. It was last-minute, and all I could think
about was getting something to drink and going to the
bathroom."

He nodded knowingly. "I knew you were doing the
display window again."

"How?" Had she missed him in the crowd tonight?
God knew she'd been looking.

"That ridiculous way you were dressed. Tom and I
figured it out." He chuckled. "I can't imagine what kind

of display you were doing. I wanted to swing by and have a look, but I had to meet a client for dinner. Besides, I didn't want to embarrass you, either."

She looked down at her tightly clasped hands, wondering what happened to that speech she'd spent two hours rehearsing. Not a speech, really, just a few sentences. She figured she couldn't handle much more.

"Take Horn's offer," Eric said, covering both her hands with one of his. "And you won't have to do any more of those windows or dress like that again. You're better than that, Dallas."

She stiffened, and he leaned forward to lightly kiss her lips. She let him, even though she didn't appreciate what he'd said. After he sat back again, she bit her lip and stared down at her lap. If she looked him in the eyes, she'd get all jumbled up.

"Dallas?"

She looked up into his anxious eyes and swallowed. "Kiss me."

"What?"

"Kiss me again. Please."

He smiled and, leaning toward her, cupped the back of her neck. Their lips met, and she put more enthusiasm into this kiss—enough that his ardent response made her a little dizzy. Made her chicken. But she had no choice. No more fantasy life. This was the end of the line.

She wasn't sure who broke the kiss. They both kind of leaned back at the same time and looked at each other. The only other two sitting at the bar, on the opposite end, let out a howl. Apparently one of the baseball teams had scored. Dallas glanced up at the screen and saw that the game had ended.

"You're not going to accept Horn's offer," he said in a flat voice.

Her gaze went to him. He didn't look happy. "I'm sorry if that screws you up."

"Are you going to tell me why you won't consider it?"

"I did consider it and I've decided it's not the right path for me to take."

"Maybe we should discuss this further. I don't think you realize what kind of opportunity this is. Horn is very influential in the business community. He has deep pockets and he loves to spend money on advertising."

"Look, Eric, I do understand and I'm flattered that you both want me for this position, but I already have a job, and—"

"I told you that working around your schedule is no problem."

She smiled sadly and then looked away. "I don't exactly have the kind of image Horn wants."

"Are you kidding? You're perfect."

Oh, God, this was so hard. "You know how I was dressed earlier?"

He nodded and then laughed, shook his head.

"That wasn't about a window display. That's me. The real me."

"What are you talking about?"

She swallowed. "I had just gotten off work when you saw me."

"No, you were going to work. You did a window display tonight."

"Yes, but that was a favor for a friend. I believe I'd told you I haven't been in modeling for a while now." She hated watching the confusion draw his face into a frown. Hated knowing she was about to end the fantasy forever.

Her stomach was in one big knot, and she swore she was going to be sick if she didn't hurry and get this over with. But all the carefully chosen words she'd practiced wouldn't come to mind. And every bit of it was her fault. She should have told him the moment he'd made the offer. Before he'd seen her dressed in dirty overalls, carrying that stupid Aladdin lunch pail. God, if she could only start over…

Eric could see something was wrong. Seriously wrong. She could have blindfolded him to keep from seeing the anguish on her face and he would know just by the tension cramping the muscles in his shoulders and the back of his neck.

He silently cleared his throat and reached for her hand. It was cold and she immediately drew back. "Dallas, you're obviously upset. Whatever's wrong, I'm sure we can fix it."

She shook her head. "It's not a matter of fixing it. I'm not a model. I don't have a glamorous job. I'm a construction worker. Garden variety. That's it."

"What?" He started to laugh, until he saw that she was serious. "But you have a graduate degree."

"Yes," she said flatly.

He stared, waiting, expecting this to be part of the joke. "You're serious," he said finally.

Her lips twisted in a wry smile. "I wouldn't make up something like this."

"Why?"

"Why have I chosen to work in construction?"

He nodded, not knowing what to say yet juggling a dozen questions in his mind. Hard to reconcile the gorgeous woman sitting in front of him with the one he saw on the street earlier.

"It started out as an accident. After I quit modeling, I signed up with a temporary agency and they sent me on a laborer's job. I have to admit I was somewhat appalled at first, but it was kind of kicky, you know? Doing something so incredibly different. And the pay sure beat typing or answering phones or filling a clerical position."

Another piece of the puzzle fell into place. "And your parents hated it."

Sighing, she briefly looked down at her hands. "Childish, I know."

He took a sip of his scotch, letting silence stretch, trying to figure out where this left them. Personally nothing had to change. After all, what did they have besides sex?

At that undeniable truth, anger gripped him. Anger at her for not being honest with him. Anger with himself for caring.

God, what a mess. He had to hold it together, though. He still had Horn's account to worry about.

"Okay," he said finally, his mind starting to clear. "Frankly I don't see a problem. Horn's offer will mean a lot more money, and you've already had your juvenile fling."

Flinching, she looked at him with such a wounded expression, he immediately regretted his words.

"Look, I didn't mean to sound snide." He pushed a hand through his hair, glanced around for the bartender, but then quickly decided another drink might not be wise. "Let's start over." He smiled.

Dallas didn't. She sighed and shook her head. "Let's save us both the grief. There's nothing you can say to make me change my mind. I can't accept Horn's offer."

"Because of me?"

She laughed softly. "It has nothing to do with you."

"Why then?"

"It's complicated."

"I have time."

She picked up her club soda and took a thoughtful sip. "I have a question." Avoiding his intense gaze, she paused to put down the glass. And then she looked him directly in the eyes. "Does this change anything between us?"

He cleared his throat, tried to maintain eye contact but ended up briefly looking away. "What do you mean?"

A sad smile slowly curved the corners of her mouth. "That's what I thought."

"Hey—"

She pulled some money out of her purse, laid it on the bar and slid off the stool.

"Dallas, wait, you didn't let me finish."

"Good luck with Horn's account, Eric. I mean it."
She leaned over to kiss him briefly on the cheek and
then she left.

_18_

"YOU'RE OUT OF YOUR MIND." Wendy set down an un-opened box of Kleenex on the floor near the pink fuzzy house slippers Dallas was wearing. "How could you turn down a job like that?"

Dallas sniffed, huddled deeper into the beanbag chair, pointed the remote at the television and turned up the volume. As if she didn't already know every word to _Pretty Woman_. Better than listening to her annoying roommate tell her what a schmuck she was.

Wendy handed her a mug of steaming chamomile tea and grabbed the remote. "Not that I don't admire your loyalty, but you'll probably end up getting fired over this insane crusade and then where will you be?"

"Thank you for your support."

"Hey, kiddo..."

At the sympathy in Wendy's voice, Dallas looked grudgingly at her. Contrary to what Wendy thought, Dallas wasn't crying. In fact, she hadn't shed a single tear. She had got what she wanted out of the fantasy. One week of bliss. The best sex she'd ever had. Now it was over. She was a big girl. She could accept that and move on.

Wendy sighed and curled up on the love seat with her

own cup of tea. "I'm on your side, remember? What kind of friend would I be if I didn't tell you that I think you're making a colossal mistake?"

"Okay, you've told me. Thank you. Now, may I please watch this movie in peace?"

"Have you discussed this with Trudie?"

Dallas groaned. "Am I not speaking clearly enough?"

"I bet she thinks you're crazy, too. Those women will be fine. Loyalty has to have a limit. Think about yourself for a change."

Dallas cursed—something she rarely did—tightened the belt to her white terry robe and struggled to her feet. She couldn't listen to Wendy another minute. Sitting alone in her bedroom without a television was better than having the big, fat mess that was her life rubbed in her face.

At the last moment she remembered the small box of Godiva truffles she'd splurged on after knocking off work and scooped it up before plodding down the short hall to her room. Wendy made a comment about Dallas stuffing her face with chocolate not being the solution right before she closed the bedroom door with a deliberate click. Forget about it. She didn't understand. Nobody did.

Even with the air conditioner on, her room was warm and sticky, and she threw off her robe. After carelessly shoving her quilt to the foot of the bed, she stretched out in her bra and panties and stared at the ceiling. Almost as if it magnetically drew her, her gaze went to her cell phone. The message light blinked.

Knowing it was Eric, she forced her gaze away. He'd called three times since last night. She hadn't picked up once. She didn't have anything to say. Anything he wanted to hear, anyway. It was over. She'd seen the look on his face when she'd asked if anything had changed between them. He hadn't needed to say a word after that.

She didn't blame him. In his business, they called what she'd done "false advertising." She'd worn the pretty clothes, the makeup, the whole thing. She'd become exactly the type of woman he wanted. But that wasn't her. Maybe once. Not now. Not for a long time.

Of course, she'd never expected things to go this far. The fantasy was supposed to have been for one night. And then it had stretched into two, and before she knew it, she'd spent over a week with him. He'd even met her parents.

Oh, God. She covered her face and groaned.

What the hell had she been thinking?

It all seemed so complicated. Maybe she needed to see a shrink. Seriously. Because she could deny it all she wanted, but there was still that part of her that wanted to wear the makeup and the dresses and snatch that incredible contract that would put her right back in the game. That didn't put her in the same category as Wendy. Dallas hadn't chased the elusive dream. It had fallen in her lap.

And then there was Eric. She liked him. Really liked him, damn it. Not because of the sex, which was beyond totally awesome. He made her laugh and he'd been a good sport about meeting her family. A lot of guys would have stopped at the sex part. Told her she was crazy for even suggesting dinner with the folks.

Her cell phone rang, startling her, and she bolted up and almost automatically grabbed it. Instead she peered at the caller ID. It was Trudie. Absurdly disappointed, she lay back down. It wasn't as if she wanted to talk to Eric or even wanted him to call again. In fact, she didn't want to talk to anyone. Not even Trudie.

All she wanted to do was wallow in self-pity for a while. Lick her wounds in private. Be alone with her scary thoughts. And wish she'd never met Horn. Or Eric Harmon.

ERIC SAT AT HIS DESK, STARING at his phone. Three days, and she hadn't called. Not once. Hadn't returned his messages. Not even to tell him to go to hell. This was starting to get to him. He wasn't the one who'd orchestrated the charade.

And contrary to what she assumed, he didn't care what she did for a living. He'd been surprised. Okay, shocked. And then confused and hurt. Yeah, they hadn't known each other long, but why couldn't she have told him? Why the big secret?

Granted, he might have been a little turned off if he'd found out when he'd first met her. Curious, certainly, but not seriously interested.

Tom stopped at his office door, glanced over his shoulder and said, "Webber's on the warpath. Horn just called him and wants to know why you're avoiding him."

"Hell, I'm not avoiding him. I told him I didn't have an answer yet."

"Just wanted to give you a heads-up, buddy." Tom slid another look down the hall before frowning at Eric. "You okay?"

"Fine."

"You don't look so good."

"Yeah." Eric scrubbed his face, exhaled slowly. He hadn't slept worth a damn the past two nights. His thoughts were never far from Dallas. How could she possibly prefer her construction job to the opportunity Horn offered? Maybe she simply didn't understand the magnitude of Horn's offer.

If she invested wisely, after her three-year contract expired, she wouldn't have to work for a while. Take time off to figure out what she wanted to do, start her own business, do whatever... So many options would be available to her if she'd only call him back.

"You wanna go to lunch?" Tom studied him with genuine concern. "Might be a good time to get out of here and clear your head before the old man calls you in."

"No, thanks." He got up, grabbed his suit jacket off his credenza.

Tom looked confused, his gaze following Eric's movements as he shrugged on the jacket. "Am I missing something?"

"I need to run an errand."

"Want company?"

Eric shook his head.

"Anything I can do?"

Eric paused. "Stall Horn. Get him off my back. Tell him I'll have a final answer for him by tomorrow."

"Will you?"

"I sure as hell hope so."

ERIC LEFT TRUDIE'S OFFICE feeling less optimistic than when he'd gone in. Just locating her had been a feat in itself. He'd started with the human resource department, who'd claimed no knowledge of Dallas. Nor had customer service. And not the security officer, who, he was pretty sure, had thought Eric was a stalker. By the time he'd gotten a lead on Trudie and convinced her to talk to him, he'd almost given up.

Might as well have done just that. The problem was bigger than he'd thought, and he had no idea how to fix it.

At the intersection he glanced at his watch. Too early to go to Pete's for a drink, which he certainly didn't need anyway, considering the obstacle he faced. But he didn't want to go back to the office, either. Not until he had a chance to think this through.

He headed down Lexington in the direction of his apartment. Normally he'd take a cab, but he figured the walk might help clear his head. Damn it. Any other reason Dallas had for turning down the offer he could poke holes in. But loyalty? He didn't have a chance. Not with this woman.

He smiled at the irony of the situation. Hell, the whole mess was one big irony. The very thing he admired her for doing was going to screw him to the wall. And then there was Capshaw's Construction—biggest outfit in the tristate area and the company who'd built most of Horn's malls. They had her, and Horn wanted her. If Eric could only figure out a way for her to keep her promise to her friends and still accept Horn's contract. Keep her from letting her career go down the damn tubes.

As much as he admired and respected her loyalty, it wasn't going to make a damn bit of difference. The union wouldn't help, and Capshaw's was too big a company to worry about a handful of disgruntled employees. Yeah, they'd make nice, say all the right things because they were obligated to legally, but when it came down to it, on the job, the men wouldn't be admonished for their behavior if it cost production time.

Eric had seen those scenarios back in Pittsburgh. It had always bothered him when his father used to defend these guys—good old boys.

Damn, what the hell was he going to do? He had to think, slow down his spinning thoughts, or he'd be useless. At an intersection he almost stepped off the curb too soon and got plowed down by a green Honda.

This wasn't just about her job. Or his, for that matter. This was about them. It was soon, their relationship was only budding, but he knew there was something there, something they could build on if they both didn't get too prideful or stupid.

He glanced at his watch. Maybe he should catch a cab the rest of the way. He didn't have a lot of time. As helpful as Trudie had been, she still wouldn't give him information on how to reach Dallas. But Trudie had given him a lead. Dallas would be in the display window tomorrow night. So whatever he came up with, it had better be quick.

DALLAS POSITIONED HERSELF IN the window at the white vanity table that had been preset for the bedroom scene. She was going to kill Trudie. No wonder the coward had had her assistant meet Dallas with wardrobe and instructions. A red negligee. What the hell was she thinking?

Of course, it wasn't too revealing, thanks to flesh-colored tape. They had to keep the window PG rated, after all, but still… What if Eric were to come by again?

The unnerving thought had her furtively scanning the growing crowd. Hell, he probably didn't want to see her, either. The calls had already stopped. She hadn't had a message or even a missed call from him since last night. He sure had given up easily. Even though it wasn't a surprise, it still disappointed her. More than that, depressed her. What a week they'd had. She'd had such hopes….

She couldn't think about him. If she did, her face would show too much expression and movement, and the scene would be ruined. As much as Trudie was going to hear about this particular getup, Dallas didn't want to spoil her high. The windows apparently had been wildly successful resulting in skyrocketing sales, and her boss had given her a promotion and raise. In fact, he was so pleased, he wanted them to continue. Trudie had the idea of a continuing-soap-opera theme and wanted Dallas to consider working for her part-time.

What a joke. Of course, she may need the money after she got fired from Capshaw's Construction.

She almost blinked. Had to force her mind to go blank. Wrong time to think about the letter or anything else that was about to mess up her pathetic life.

For the next two hours she managed to stay on track by mentally reviewing her grocery list, her Christmas list—anything innocuous enough to keep the crazy thoughts away. Even without her watch, she knew it was close to time for a break. She was thirsty and her left leg kept wanting to fall asleep.

Behind her she heard someone at the window door and waited for her cue to move. That's when she saw him. Eric stood at the edge of the small crowd. Her heart threatened to leap from her chest. If she didn't hear her cue in the next three seconds, she was going to take matters into her own hands. She tried like hell to look away, but her gaze stayed on him.

In his right hand he held a briefcase, yet he wore jeans and a white polo shirt. His expression was partially hidden in a shadow, so she couldn't read him. Behind her someone gave her the okay to step back, and when she moved, so did Eric. Straight for the door.

She almost fell on her face in her haste to beat him. Once she got out and made it to the back of the store and through the employees' door, she'd be safe. If he had the nerve to follow, security would stop him. Not that she wanted to make a scene, but she couldn't deal with him right now.

She grabbed the robe offered by Trudie's assistant

and then headed for the back of the store without wasting a single second by glancing over her shoulder. She had at least a thirty-second lead and headed the most direct route to the back. Not until she reached the employee door did she turn around. Several people huddled around the customer service desk, and a woman with a yawning toddler browsed the stationery. But no sign of him. Had he given up that easily again?

With equal measures of disappointment and relief she turned back to push through the door. Instead she met a familiar broad chest. "Eric, what are you doing here?"

"You won't answer my calls."

"I can't talk right now." She pulled the robe sash tighter.

"Then when?"

"Later."

"It's important, Dallas. I really have to talk to you tonight. I'll need an answer for Horn right away."

She sighed. If he didn't look so earnest, she'd be angry. "There's nothing more to discuss," she said softly. "My hands are tied."

"I know."

Something in the resignation in his voice made her believe he did. She glanced around and then asked, "What do you know?"

"I talked to Trudie."

"You what?"

He sighed heavily, and for the first time she noticed how exhausted he looked. Lines radiated from the corners of his eyes, and the lines bracketing his mouth were exaggerated. "You wouldn't return my calls. I had to do something."

"What did she tell you?" Anger raised her voice a little, and she had to take a deep breath.

"What you should have. About the letter you're writing."

"Don't you lecture me."

He smiled. "I'm not. I think what you're doing is admirable. But if you don't give me a few minutes to show you the new ad I came up with for Horn, then I will turn you over my knee."

She laughed. She couldn't help it. "Look, I know you mean well, but—"

"I won't lecture you if you don't patronize me. Just listen to what I have to say, damn it."

Dallas grabbed his wrist to look at his watch. "I have only ten minutes left. Let's see if we can use Trudie's office."

She led him through the door, her heart pounding just knowing he was right behind her. He didn't have a solution, she knew. He couldn't possibly, but that he was here, that he was still interested, was something.

Trudie wasn't there, but her door was open and Dallas took the liberty of taking Eric inside and closing the door. He didn't waste any time in propping his briefcase on the desk and snapping it open.

"In the interest of time, I'll cut to the chase. Capshaw's Construction does a lot of Horn's work, mostly malls catering to middle-class families. He's moving more and more outside of the city into the tristate area and he needs to appeal to different kinds of people."

He took out a sketch pad and flipped it open. "What I've done is to incorporate the two companies in the campaign, showing them working together to better the community. I've taken some liberties," he said with a cocky grin as he showed her the first sketch of buildings under construction in the background and a female worker in the forefront.

She stared in surprise. "That's supposed to be me?"

"Nope. One of the others. I understand you have quite a network of women working construction." He flipped to the next page, again featuring a female construction worker at work—a bit more glamorous than was realistic, but still...

"I figure we could use the different women for different billboards, print ads, commercial spots. Capshaw's can't turn it down. Horn is a large part of their bread and butter. Besides, it puts Capshaw's in a better light than they deserve."

"And they'd be forced to play the part of concerned employer," she muttered, still a little dazed by it all.

"Exactly. Interested?"

"Horn's not going to go for this."

"I already pitched it to him."

"What?" She gripped the edge of Trudie's desk. "He wants it?"

"He's thinking about it. But I believe I've made a good case for him to court the suburbs differently than he's courted the city." He paused. "There is a catch. You have to be part of the package."

She'd already figured that out. She'd end up being his rep in the city, doing the glamorous shots. What she didn't know was how much this effort had been about pleasing his client or about smoothing things for them. "You took an awful chance."

He shrugged. "It's a good business idea. Brilliant on my part, really," he said, grinning, but then sobered just as quickly. "And I admire what you're doing for these women. You could walk away and make a bundle." He grinned again. "You're what we call a stand-up guy."

"All right. No butch jokes."

"Not from me. Think your friends will go for it?"

"Oh, yeah. I can't wait to see the guys' faces when they find out." She realized she'd spoken out loud. "The guys we work with who give us a bad time. Their jaws are going to drop."

He nodded. "Want to see the rest of the sketches?"

"Sure." This was terrific. The women would have to be excited. And so was Dallas. She was grateful, too, but it was dampened by this tiny niggling suspicion that Eric had orchestrated this to get her out of the construction business. No big deal in the larger scheme of things. But it was there.

He flipped through a few more pages and then paused before showing her the last one. "The thing is, you might have to keep your day job. The money won't be as much, since it has to be spread around."

"No problem."

He showed her the final page. "What do you think?"

She stared in disbelief. It was her. In coveralls, carrying the silly Aladdin lunch pail. She started laughing, horribly afraid she might end up crying.

"You okay?"

She nodded. "Kiss me."

He tossed the pad aside and pulled her into his arms. His mouth touched hers and his gentleness made her want to weep.

She didn't have to ask where this turn of events left them. She'd found it in his kiss.

Epilogue

"I THINK THIS BLUSH might be too dark. What do you think?" Nancy asked, staring into the mirror with a critical eye.

Before Dallas could answer, the photographer shook his head impatiently and said, "It's perfect. Let's get in place for this shoot."

Dallas stepped back, out of the way, and watched him set up the scene, feeling like a proud mama. Nancy and the rest of the women had really blossomed in the past two months, their confidence and self-esteem soaring. Old man Capshaw treated them like gold, which sure helped.

"Hey."

At the sound of Eric's voice she turned around. "Hey."

He kissed her briefly. "How's it going?"

"Terrific. This afternoon I'll be reviewing the new contracts with Dakota. I'm getting a family discount. I'll owe her dinner."

He smiled. "What a deal. Have you told the rest of your family about your new career direction?"

"Yep. They think I'll make the perfect agent." She knew her mother had hoped for something different, but she was being supportive and Dallas appreciated that. "Of course, right now my job is easy. Everyone's thrilled with being in the spotlight. But I know it won't always be this simple, and I'm looking forward to the challenge."

Eric took her hand and with his thumb, stroked the inside of her wrist. His voice lowered, and he said, "I'm looking forward to tonight."

Holding back a smile, she arched her brows. "And what would that be?"

"Want me to show you?" He tugged at her hand.

She laughed, and shot a glance at the photographer and Nancy. "You wouldn't dare."

"No?"

The simple whispered word, the slightest curve of his mouth was all he needed to turn her to putty. She sighed. Yep, life was perfect.

* * * * *

Watch for Debbi Rawlins's appearance in the hot,
new Blaze miniseries,
DO NOT DISTURB
Coming in December 2005!